Anne E. Steinke

CHEERLEADERS

22

Rivals

Hippo Books
Scholastic Publications Limited
London

Scholastic Publications Ltd.,
10 Earlham Street, London WC2H 9RX, UK

Scholastic Inc.,
730 Broadway, New York, NY 10003, USA

Scholastic Tab Publications Ltd.,
123 Newkirk Road, Richmond Hill,
Ontario L4C 3G5, Canada

Ashton Scholastic Pty. Ltd.,
PO Box 579, Gosford, New South Wales,
Australia

Ashton Scholastic Ltd.,
165 Marua Road, Panmure, Auckland 6,
New Zealand

First published by Scholastic Inc., USA, 1986
First published in the UK by Scholastic Publications
Ltd., 1987

Copyright © Ann E. Steinke, 1986

ISBN 0 590 70783 3

All rights reserved

Made and printed by Cox & Wyman, Reading, Berks

This book is sold subject to the condition that it shall not,
by way of trade or otherwise be lent, resold, hired out, or
otherwise circulated without the publisher's prior
consent in any form of binding or cover other than that in
which it is published and without a similar condition,
including this condition, being imposed upon the
subsequent purchaser.

CHAPTER

Ardith looked at her new squad and wanted to resign. Was it just one week ago they had all been at the cabin she'd taken them to so they could get used to working together? By the end of the week it had really looked like they were beginning to be a united group.

But now. Just look at them, she thought, feeling defeated. They appeared so mentally isolated they practically had glass domes around themselves. With the possible exception of Hope Chang and Peter Rayman. They were more or less sitting side by side on the gym risers, facing her, looking attentive. The others were attentive, true, but in a remote sort of way.

Tara Armstrong, her long red hair cascading gracefully over her shoulders, sat there looking as if she expected to be crowned queen imminently.

Jessica Bennett seemed distracted, perhaps

even troubled. Her green eyes definitely had a faraway look.

Sean Dubrow, the king of Hunkdom, had a bored expression on his face. It looked like the week between their stay at the cabin and today, the second day of school, had undone any positive work accomplished on his character and attitude. Ardith had thought Pres Tilford had been a handful the year before. Sean made Pres look like an angel sometimes.

And Olivia Evans.

More than anybody, Ardith had counted on Olivia, the one remaining member from last season's Varsity Squad, to look like she was raring to go, ready to take charge and make the new squad the best ever. Instead, she looked like she was about to be sick.

What Ardith had to do was give this bunch some kind of incentive, a shot in the arm, to really excite them and get them moving.

Suddenly, in a flash of brilliance, she had it. Out with the old, in with the new. That old adage just might save this group.

"All right, everyone. I hope your week off has left you rested and ready to work really hard this year. I've been thinking" — for all of about thirty seconds, she thought drolly — "about a way to keep this squad from being a carbon copy of the old one. I want you to stand out on your own, to be appreciated by the Tarenton fans for *who* you are, not simply *what* you are."

The six cheerleaders were eyeing her with vari-

2

ous expressions of puzzlement. She cut the rhetoric and jumped right in.

"Even though you've just spent a week learning them, we're tossing out the old routines. We're going to be devising brand-new cheers — routines that will showcase the unique talent each of you has. I've got a few ideas of my own and I'm assigning each of you to come up with at least one fresh idea by tomorrow afternoon's practice." She looked at all of them, trying to gauge their reactions.

For once Sean failed to look bored. Who knew what he was thinking? Ardith didn't care. As long as that cocky, make-my-day look was gone from his face, she felt relieved.

What Sean was thinking was that Ardith had just given him an assignment that he could parlay into a chance to demonstrate his worth. He'd use his considerable skill as a dancer, combined with his undeniable athletic ability, to dream up the best routine this old school had ever seen. This would give him an excuse not to do his homework tonight, too. Well, at least not right away.

Tara sat even taller. Wow! Here was a way for her to shine. Working up a new routine that would blow the crowd away was a surefire way to make everyone really appreciate what an asset she was to the squad. If she couldn't be the best gymnast on the Varsity Squad, she could be an inspired choreographer of great cheering moves!

Jessica stretched her slender legs, feeling itchy to be on the move. She liked the idea of being

3

asked to come up with a cheerleading routine, but she just hoped the argument that had started this morning at home would have died down by now so she could have some peace and quiet in the family room for inventing something.

Hope slid Peter a look. She was wondering if he realized what a gift Ardith had just handed them. Here was the perfect chance for Peter to show himself as someone with a special talent that would benefit the squad. Hope had no illusions about her own ability to dream up a cheer; hers would probably only rank as adequate. But she had complete faith in Peter since he'd demonstrated back in the spring during tryouts that he was more than capable of inventing snappy routines. She smiled at Peter, and caught his eye.

Peter was not entertaining quite such positive thoughts. If he could peg Dubrow right, he knew that guy would knock himself out to be nothing less than spectacular. Peter wasn't so sure that he himself could be spectacular with only one night to work up a routine. But he'd have to try. He wasn't about to lie down and simply let Sean blow him away. If it took all night, he'd come up with the best routine in cheerleading history.

Olivia had gone into shock. Toss out the old squad's routines as if they were so much garbage? And *she* was supposed to come up with a new routine that might replace one of the perfectly good old ones? She looked around at the other cheerleaders, who suddenly resembled strangers.

Olivia, who just the year before, as a new

4

cheerleader, had had to get used to five new people, felt her attitude changing and decided, despite the experiences up at the lake, that she did not want to do it again. I shouldn't feel this way, she tried to tell herself. I'm a full year older; I should be more mature, more equal to the challenge. Besides, I'm *captain*. But I don't want to make up a new cheer!

She heard herself whining just like a spoiled child, "But, the old cheers were terrific, Mrs. Engborg."

It was bad enough she had to learn to get along with five new people, all of whom she wasn't even sure at this point she liked very much. Now she was supposed to get used to a whole host of brand-new cheers? It was too much. It was overkill. She didn't want to do it.

Ardith raised an eyebrow and looked at Olivia, who sat perched on the bottom riser looking like a beaten puppy. What was the matter with that girl?

Olivia's deepset brown eyes darkened even more as she caught the coach's look.

"I mean, some of those routines weren't just good — they were great. How can you improve on that? And that routine we devised at the last minute that won us the Tri-State championship was . . . was — well, we won!" she stated as if that said it all.

Ardith took a deep breath, aware that the five other members of the squad were shifting uneasily and exchanging glances. She nodded briskly and agreed. "True. So that's why coming up with new stuff will really be a whopper of a challenge."

She concentrated on the others, unwilling to see Olivia's stricken expression any longer. The girl needed time, that was all. She'd appeared to get herself together up at the cabin. The week off must have been detrimental for her, but now that school was in session and she'd be involved in cheerleading practice and games, she'd perk up.

Olivia stared at Ardith. Sometimes she felt that Mrs. Engborg was like a boulder. She was that solid, that unmovable. When she made up her mind about something, forget trying to get her to change it. And now she'd decided to reject the old squad's material. Olivia was a member of the old squad, so she felt like Ardith was rejecting her, too.

Ardith was talking again and Olivia fought her way up through the abysmal depths of her emotions to try to listen.

"Now, there's another change I've decided to make on a permanent basis. As you all may know, from what you experienced two weeks ago, cheerleading isn't child's play. It's hard, physically demanding work. And it's especially stressful to have to shoulder the full responsibility, as Olivia has had, of doing all the more acrobatic stunts.

"Since we have two great gymnasts on the squad this year, I've decided to divide up that responsibility equally so we can use both to the best advantage. Jessica and Olivia will share the burden of executing the intricate flips and jumps, et cetera, that are required from time to time.

6

This will allow Olivia to have a break and relieve some of her tension and stress."

Ardith looked at Jessica to see how she felt about that. The girl's expression had definitely changed for the better. No longer looking distracted, she looked eager to work, to get at it, and start practicing some of those elaborate, gravity-defying cheers.

Almost reluctantly, Ardith switched her attention to observe Olivia's reaction. She expected to see — what? Relief? An ease of tension on the girl's pinched face? What she saw was far from it.

Olivia felt as if a tight metal band were squeezing her chest, crushing all the breath and life out of her. If she'd felt Ardith's rejection before, that had been nothing compared to what she felt now. She felt as if Ardith had walked up to her, slapped her across the face, and sent her packing.

Not to be the gymnastic star anymore? Relinquish that role? She realized her fear of Jessica had been founded on solid ground all along. Jessica had become Ardith's darling. While she, Olivia, was a has-been. Ardith might mask her rejection by calling it a break, an easing of tension and stress, but Olivia knew it wasn't that at all. She'd been replaced. Like a worn-out sweater. Like a —

She had to pull herself together. She had to stop being so maudlin and childish. She forced herself to smile tightly at Ardith, in acknowledgement of her decision. After all, she was squad captain and it was up to her to at least *look* like she supported Ardith's decisions.

7

Ardith looked only slightly convinced. She turned away and walked with that firm, energetic step of hers out about ten feet onto the maple floor of the gym. She pirouetted smartly and said, "Okay, now for the first idea for one of our brand-new cheers."

CHAPTER

2

Music reverberated off the gym walls. The heavy beat of a Springsteen number was accented by six sets of fists punching into the air. Ardith's clear voice sounded out the count as the cheerleaders attempted to get into step. They were working on a sideline cheer that Ardith hoped would whip the Tarenton fans into a high-energy response. Words had only been roughly devised to accompany the cheer, but no one was using them at the moment anyway. Ardith despaired of ever getting that far. It seemed impossible enough trying to get twelve legs to step, swing, kick, and jump in unison.

"Okay," she called. "On the count of five you swing like opening doors to the left, left leg stationary, right leg stiff, arms outstretched in a V. One, two, three, four, five!" She suppressed a groan as she watched.

9

Olivia again. Slow on the count. And Hope, turning on four. What was with these six? She knew her squad didn't drink or use drugs, and she expected them to not stay out late at night. It was like training for the football team: They were supposed to be in peak condition, both physically and mentally. Instead they acted like they were ready for a convalescent home.

Ardith glanced at the clock. Only half an hour to go. Please let me keep calm, she prayed. "All right. From the top. Let's run through it again. One, two. . . ."

Olivia tried to concentrate. Sideline cheers. What a waste of a good squad. She'd always liked them the least. She turned on five to her left and stared at the back of Sean's handsome head. Of course, all of him was handsome. Too bad he was so full of himself. Pres had never been so conceited. And Walt, Walt Manners, her co-cheerleader and boyfriend. Oh, Walt! She bit her lip painfully to force herself to listen to Ardith's instructions.

Jessica, on the other side of Sean, felt his eyes staring at her. She supposed he would like to date her but she felt curiously immune to his animal magnetism. Fully four-fifths of the girls in school rubbernecked in the halls when he sauntered by. His self-centered type just didn't attract Jessica. I'll take a man who likes to have fun, who doesn't expect adoration.

Before Jessica could decide who could fill the requirements, Ardith called, "Break!" She spoke the words as if she wanted every bone in their collective bodies to do just that. Had they been that pitiful?

Tara leaned way over, her curly red hair falling around her upside-down head, to try to get the blood back into her brain. She was beginning to feel like a human top, what with all the turning and spinning Ardith was making them do. Would this cheer ever look any good when they'd gotten it down? She decided she'd figure out some kind of jazz-inspired sideline cheer that would be a vast improvement on Ardith's. No doubt Mrs. Engborg was a good coach, and a true athlete in her own right, but she was old. Over forty, for heaven's sake! Out of it. She didn't have the slightest idea of how to inspire teenagers. But Tara did, and she'd zap them tomorrow with her little routine.

Sean took advantage of the break to lie back on an exercise mat and study Tara through half-closed eyes. Even in repose, his well-muscled body inspired admiration and he was aware of it.

Tara, now *she* had potential, Sean thought. Jessica clearly wasn't interested in him — for now. That irritated him a little. He was used to girls falling all over themselves to get his attention. He didn't like holdouts. But a whole year stretched ahead of them. He and Jessica would practice five afternoons a week and participate in every game. She'd have plenty of time in which to get to know him. Sean was positive that with patience and perseverance he'd crack Jessica's veneer and she'd be his for the asking.

As for Olivia, he'd given her an unsuccessful

try back in the spring, but besides that she was so down on everything right now that *he* wasn't interested in her. And Hope obviously had the hots for scarecrow Rayman. How a guy that skinny had the strength to hoist girls around like he did was a mystery. Sheer willpower, probably.

So back to Tara. Beautiful for sure. A party pooper, though. He couldn't believe she'd been such a dud when he'd wanted to have some fun in town while they'd been at the cabin. She'd probably been afraid of Ardith's wrath. Sean smiled to himself. He had to admit, her wrath was considerable. But get Tara away from Mrs. E., back here in Tarenton, and she might have potential. He didn't doubt for a moment that once he made up his mind he wanted Tara, she'd be his. Who in this school could possibly compete with him?

"Okay, kids. Enough taking it easy. Up on your feet and let's try to get the routine right from the *beginning* to the *end* before six o'clock." Ardith clapped her hands, and the cheerleaders rose to their feet, looking tired and without even the zest needed to cheer a rat on through a maze. They lined up: Hope, Peter, Tara, Olivia, Sean, and Jessica. Ardith, who'd rewound the tape, punched the on button and began counting. "One, two, three. . . ."

The six cheerleaders, the best the school had to offer, really tried this time. Twelve legs swung "like doors" exactly on the count of five, followed by high kicks to the left with their right legs swinging over their bodies, hands doing a straight-armed clap over their heads; then back to a leg-spread stance, arms at their sides and ending with a high C jump. The balance required to execute the three basic stages was achieved by the six perfectly tuned bodies, and when Ardith beamed at them, they smiled back in relief.

"Excellent," she said in the voice of someone who'd just witnessed a miracle. Tension eased from her face as she continued. "Now, don't forget. Tomorrow I want to see some outstanding routines. Refer to your cheerleading handbook for the types of moves you think would be just right. If we don't know them now, we'll learn them." She walked over to shut off the tape recorder.

The six cheerleaders disbanded as if they really weren't a squad, but just happened to be in the same place at the same time, and wandered haphazardly toward the gym doors leading to the hallway. The two guys headed for the boys' locker room, Sean, as always, striding ahead. Peter Rayman glared at his back. He really hated that macho, superior attitude that Sean put on some of the time. What Sean Dubrow needed was to be taken down a peg — a dozen of them, in fact. Peter wished he had the way to do it. Peter knew that last year's squad seemed to have been friendly; even the two guys, Walt and Pres, had seemed to like each other. He also knew that squad unity was essential for smooth execution of the cheers, but he didn't see how in the world he and Sean would *ever* be unified in anything other than mutual dislike. Hope watched Peter slouch down the hall in Sean's wake. She was aware that he resented Sean, but couldn't understand why. As a cheerleader, Peter was just as good as Sean. As a person he was better, since he had more humanity, less egotism. Sean walked around as if he *owned* the world; Peter walked around as if he were *supporting* the world. It wasn't fair! Could she do something to relieve the weight from Peter's shoulders?

Shrugging glumly, she followed the other girls into the locker room.

Tara's pleasant, musical voice was babbling away. Hope had to admire a girl who never seemed to be at a loss for words. Sometimes she couldn't think of anything to say. Small talk. Her small talk was so small it was miniscule.

"It's really a shame that cheer Ardith's got us doing doesn't involve any special gymnastic stunts for you and Olivia," Tara was remarking to Jessica. "I mean, it's such a *boring* cheer."

"Oh, I don't know," Jessica said, pulling her white practice sweat shirt over her head. "If we could just get *together* and do it right, and bring in the words, I think it'll be dramatic. Like a chorus line on Broadway."

"Hmmm, maybe." Tara didn't look the least bit convinced. "Still, it doesn't exactly *showcase* your talents. I'm going to work up a routine that will do that." She smiled widely at Jessica and waited.

"Oh, you've got an idea already?" Jessica stripped off the hot pink sweats from her legs and

14

lifted her sparkling green gaze to Tara in-quiringly.

"I've *always* got ideas," Tara said with a tin-kling laugh, and trotted off to the showers.

I'll just bet you do, Olivia thought, and closed her locker door with more force than needed. She didn't feel like staying afterward to shower and change. Besides, this new bunch of girls hadn't seen the faint scars that crossed her chest from the heart surgery she'd had as a child, and she wasn't ready to start displaying herself to them. If she ever would be. Tossing her books into her gym bag on top of her discarded school clothes, Olivia left the locker room without saying any-thing to anybody.

Hope watched her go, a troubled look on her face.

CHAPTER

Jessica Bennett approached her house with caution. By now it was six-thirty and she knew her mom and stepfather would be home waiting dinner on her. The appearance of the house was deceptive, she was thinking. So peaceful looking from the outside, so unruffled a facade. Wasn't it curious how at times so much turmoil could lurk behind such a placid exterior?

Jessica hugged her books closer to her chest as if she were going to use them to ward off an assailant. Sometimes she wished she were a stranger to the occupants of that house and could just walk on by — glance at the house and objectively admire it, and then proceed down the street to her real destination. A place where she knew her entrance through the front door wouldn't start a resurgence of hostilities.

Why couldn't her stepfather understand? Why

did he have to measure everything she did as a teenager with a yardstick meant for staid adults? Why couldn't her mother have picked a man who knew how to deal with a family? Then she realized she was being uncharitable and snuffed out that line of thought.

Her pace slowed as she neared the cheery yellow front door with its colonial blue shutters and white trim. She gripped the polished brass handle and thought: character. What you may be about to experience will build character.

Smiling a bit, she quietly opened the door. Closing it just as carefully, Jessica cocked an ear to locate everybody, to sense moods. Oddly, the atmosphere reeked of normalcy. The faint sound of a television news program came from the family room at the back of the house. Clatters and clinks identified her mother's activity in the kitchen.

Jessica let out her breath and walked through the house to the kitchen.

"Hi, Mom," she said, coming into the room to find her mother pulling a casserole from the oven.

"Jessica! How'd practice go?" Abby's slightly troubled gaze touched on the wall clock before fixing on her only daughter.

Jessica knew her mother had been concerned that she would come home later than expected. I wouldn't dare, Jessica thought dryly. Not after that ridiculous argument this morning. She could still hear her stepfather's voice sounding tired and irritable, even at the start of the day. "We're going to have to delay dinner half an hour *every* week-

17

night until she graduates?" he'd asked.

Jessica suspected his real concern was that the half hour delayed start to dinner would mean a half hour delay to his beginning any work he'd brought home. She was sure he qualified to be labeled a "workaholic." If he sounded that tired and strung out in the morning, no wonder he was even worse by the end of the day.

"Fine," Jessica told her mother. "We started learning a new routine. Mrs. Engborg decided we're going to invent new material. In fact, each of us is supposed to make up a cheer to show her at tomorrow's practice."

"Really? I know you'll have fun doing that." Abby sounded genuinely pleased for Jessica, and she had total confidence in her daughter's abilities.

"Um, does Dan plan on working after dinner, or has he got some heavy TV viewing scheduled for tonight?" Jessica looked at her mother warily.

"I'm not sure. Why?"

"Because I'll need a place to work out my cheer. The family room is the only place big enough. Besides the garage. But it's chilly and dirty in there."

"Oh. Well, I guess we'll have to see," Abby replied, her voice giving evidence of the turmoil starting up inside. If she'd entertained hopes of an evening in which there would be no clash of wills between her husband, her daughter, and herself, they were fading now. "Wash up, please." Abby went out to the family room to call Dan to dinner.

Jessica trotted up the stairs with the graceful bounding gait that gave her cheering so much appeal. Now all she had to do was get through dinner — alive — and then hole up somewhere and concentrate on creating a winner of a routine. She bet she was the only cheerleader who was going to have to work under duress.

Hope Chang stared at the cheerleader's handbook spread open on her desk and wished it was sheet music instead. Wasn't it enough she was a cheerleader? Did she have to actually *create* cheers, too? If it were up to her she'd say something like:

> "Go, Wolves, go!
> Take 'em apart!
> Get 'em, get 'em!
> Make 'em sorry
> We ever met 'em!"

Would they like something like that? She'd accent this with a few pompon waves in the air. Maybe even a C jump. Let the guys do stag leaps; let Olivia do those splits she did so well; Jessica and Tara — well, they could cartwheel and tumble or something in the background.

Hope sighed. Her dark gaze wandered lovingly to her music stand in its niche in her closet. Ask me to play my violin at a school assembly and I'd leap for joy. But make up a cheer? Help!

But, her mother had been happy and interested

when she'd learned of Mrs. Engborg's assignment. She expected Hope to come down before bedtime to demonstrate the new cheer. Hope wished she could use piles of homework as an excuse for not getting to it, but she'd finished it in study hall and right after dinner. That's what I get for being so efficient, she thought dryly. It was now eight o'clock and she had at least until ten to come up with something.

She thought of Peter Rayman. How was he doing at creating a new cheer?

Peter lay on his bed, head encased in the earphones of a Sony Walkman so he couldn't hear any sound that could be identified with his well-meaning, but meddling, mother. He hadn't even told her about Mrs. Engborg's "assignment" to produce a cheer. He knew if he did so much as one stag leap in his room, she'd come leaping herself to see what was going on.

He closed his eyes, listening to the deep vibes of a new Starship tune. That guy could really sing! The woman wasn't bad either, considering she'd been around since the sixties. She was probably almost as old as Mrs. Engborg.

Peter scowled. That reminded him of the cheerleading routine he was supposed to be making up. Sighing, he rolled over and lifted the handbook off the floor where he'd tossed it, and thumbed through it again. C jumps, pikes, splits, stags, straddle jumps, flips, thigh stands. The list of maneuvers seemed endless. More than anything he wanted to come up with a combination that would blow Sean Dubrow's cocky assurance off the map.

Sean flung himself across the living room in a forward flip. He caught an imaginary flying body, assisted it to do a midair stationary back flip, then the two of them executed a perfect shoulder stand.

Too bad this whole routine was all imaginary. It was dynamite! When the others saw his half-time routine, they'd go wild. The squad would end up in a pyramid like he'd seen the old cheerleaders do last year, only Olivia wouldn't tumble off the top. Instead, the whole squad would disassemble in a carefully orchestrated manner so they were all standing in a circle, facing out, hands joined — Sean's to Jessica's and Tara's. Peter could have Olivia and Hope; that should make him happy.

Sean grabbed a piece of looseleaf paper and started scribbling the routine down as fast as he could remember it. There were definitely compensations for all this hard work. This routine would have him hoisting Jessica around, his muscles bunched and flexed. After the girls saw him doing this cheer, he'd have a few more entries for his little black book. Maybe he'd have to buy a second one, he thought with a lopsided grin. *Little Black Book II,* the sequel to the exciting *Book I,* by Sean Dubrow.

He laughed, showing white even teeth — teeth so straight it was impossible to believe he'd ever needed braces. It was too bad he hadn't thought up a cheer that would have both Jessica and Tara falling right into his arms. Not that he needed a *cheer* to accomplish that.

Tara. Sean wondered what she'd come up with. There was one determined girl. He bet she'd be burning the midnight oil to come up with a routine that would be the top of the line. But it'd have to be awfully good to beat out Sean's.

Tara looked in her large bedroom mirror and struck a pose. She wondered if the idea she'd thought up was the best she could do. With Jessica and Olivia appointed by Mrs. Engborg as the star gymnasts, she and Hope had to more or less stay in the background as supporters. Like backup vocalists to the rock star. Tara didn't like that. She wanted to be in the limelight. She wanted to be the one people came up to after a game to compliment on that really great cheer the squad had done when the score was tied and Tarenton needed a shot in the arm.

Tara was aware that the cheerleaders for Garrison, Tarenton's arch rival, had some stunning dancelike routines. Last year's squad had never attempted to equal Garrison's dancing skills, opting instead for gymnastic dazzle. Tara intended to remedy that situation. Her fancy footwork routine would equal, if not outdo, Garrison's best.

She flipped her red hair behind her shoulders and considered going downstairs to demonstrate her idea for her parents. Her dad was working in his study, as usual. He'd say he could take a break for his favorite daughter — his *only* daughter, she thought wryly. But she knew that all the time he'd be watching her, he'd really be thinking about trials, defenses, and courtroom scenes. Did other lawyers bring their work home so much? To the point where they seemed perpetually distracted? Just once Tara wished she could be guaranteed that her father's *mind* would be on her, as well as his eyes.

As long as she could remember, her father had been distracted by work, when he wasn't playing tennis. It came with success, she supposed. But without her father's success they wouldn't have such a great house, and all the things they had that were expensive.

Tara dismissed the vague feeling of discontent that was starting to take hold, and went downstairs. She was going to find her parents and collect them in one place — if only temporarily — and make them watch her routine. They'd adore it. She knew that. And she needed a pat on the head right now, to bolster her self-confidence.

My routine just *has* to be accepted by Mrs. Engborg tomorrow, Tara thought fervently. Or I don't know what I'll do.

CHAPTER

4

Preston Tilford III resisted the urge to race his red Porsche into the parking lot like a celebrity returning to his old stomping grounds. Grandstanding like that was for silly little high schoolers. So what was he, the graduate, doing in Tarenton High's parking lot? he asked himself. It all came down to physical attraction. And flaming red hair.

He parked the car, but not in his old, favorite spot. Some insensitive clod had parked a huge, hulking black Chevy truck, with oversized tires and enough suspension for a freight car, in it. The thing looked like an overgrown Tonka toy. Just goes to show, he thought, hopping out and carefully locking the door, graduate and your elite position in the school is usurped by an upstart.

Pres walked toward the front of the school, wondering if all the little underclassmen who'd been in awe of him last year would even recognize him. He'd kept such a high profile, he supposed they'd still remember him. And give him his due respect, he thought, laughing.

He trotted up the wide stone steps and pushed in the door. Funny, all last year, cheerleading had made his senior year of school tolerable, but he'd been anxious to get out, to graduate, to leave these "hallowed halls" forever. And here he was, not even three months later, coming back voluntarily. Which proved a point. Place a bouncy, desirable girl in front of him, and he had no willpower at all.

The grin this line of thought produced was sustained by the looks girls were giving him as he crossed the hall, heading for the gym.

"Hi, Pres," one underclassman said.

Pres was so startled that a girl had actually spoken to him, he gave her a good look. A senior this year. No longer an *under*classman. Her newly acquired status must have given her the confidence to speak to him. He gave her one of his electrifying smiles, willing to acknowledge her this year, whereas last year he wouldn't have given her the time of day. She was the exact same age of Tara Armstrong, the magnet that was pulling Pres to the gym. Pres moved on, hearing the girls whispering behind him, no doubt consumed with curiosity as to why he was there.

He paused outside the gym doors to watch the cheerleaders practice without being observed himself. Ardith was talking to them. They were lined up and seemed to be going through some kind of tryouts again. Weird. Quietly he pushed through the doors and took a seat off to the side of the risers.

"Okay, Jessica. You're next," Mrs. Engborg was saying.

Jessica came out from the lineup and started talking and doing a few maneuvers. Admiring her beautiful brown hair and striking green eyes, Pres remembered that she was great to watch in action.

"Well, I thought we could have a cheer like this for when the refs are conferring and everyone is in expectation. You know how everyone gets hyped up; I figured we could direct their energies with this." With that she began demonstrating a routine that began with three foot stomps, alternating feet, accompanied by claps. She began chanting:

"Don't need a break!
Got points to make!
Time to beat their team!
Wipe 'em out like Mr. Clean!"

She went into a jazzy routine with a lot of cartwheels and tumbles, then explained how she'd figured out a flying leap for herself and Olivia, with Peter and Sean catching them in midair.

The other cheerleaders clapped when she was through and Mrs. Engborg looked pleased. Pres was impressed. Jessica was just about the most graceful thing on legs. Her movements were smooth, eye-catching. Olivia had always struck Pres as being technically perfect, but in a high energy, jabbing sort of way. Jessica's acrobatic maneuvers were a little more fluid, less abrupt. They'd make a great pair, each complementing the other. Pres decided Mrs. Engborg had really known what she was doing when she'd picked Jessica.

"That was very nice, Jessica," Mrs. Engborg said. She looked at Sean. "Now yours."

Sean strutted out onto the floor and began demonstrating his halftime cheer. His body literally flew through the air and practically sent off sparks. Pres watched him with a growing sense of unreasonable dislike. The guy was so good! Maybe a little bit of a show-off, but he had a lot to show off. Besides seeing him at the cheerleading clinic and up at the lake, Pres had seen Sean last year in the halls, and knew girls found him irresistible. This year Sean was the resident stud. Pres had really been unseated! He frowned and watched as Sean finished his routine.

Everyone clapped enthusiastically. Mrs. Engborg said little, and then, since apparently the others had demonstrated their cheers already, she addressed the whole group.

"Well, I see I've got some innovative and imaginative people on the squad this year. You all did a fine job of thinking up cheers. But I'm not going to use any one of the cheers you've shown me — " There were various expressions of disbelief and shock, but Mrs. Engborg held up her hand. "What I mean is, I'm not going to use just *one* of your cheers. I'm going to incorporate the best elements of everyone's offering into one

27

dynamic cheer. That way, when you do it, you'll all feel you've been a part of creating it."

The six cheerleaders exchanged looks. Jessica thought this was a brilliant move on Mrs. Engborg's part to unify the group. By having them work on "their" cheer, they would all be pulling together. She just hoped it worked. She especially hoped Olivia was more pleased about this idea than she looked.

Pres glanced at Olivia and thought she looked like the pits. What was the matter with her? She should be ecstatic that Mrs. Engborg was allowing the squad members to have input this early in the season. Instead, she looked like she felt ill. He slouched back and rested against the risers behind him. Maybe she did. She couldn't possibly look worse. He frowned and listened to Mrs. Engborg.

She held up a clipboard briefly and said, "I've taken notes on your routines. Tonight I'm going to combine the elements I thought were the best into a cheer that can be performed out on the floor or field. I'll also work on an abbreviated version to be done on the sidelines. I'll mix up your chants, too.

"Now, everybody out on the floor. I want you to practice a few of the basic moves you thought up so I can see how you look doing them together."

Pres's attention shifted to Tara Armstrong as she preceded the group onto the gym floor. What a knockout! And that hair. Not since Vanessa Barlow had he seen hair quite like that. He was a goner again, going crazy over some cute female. It was pathetic. I should have more resistance, he thought. Go for an older girl, not one who's still in school. He hadn't let on that he found Tara so attractive when he'd gone up to the lake to watch the new squad practice. But Tara had been on his mind a lot this last week, so he'd decided to drop by the school to see if she was as unforgettable as he thought. Pres watched Tara's body move to Ardith's instructions. Right, old boy, he thought. Just try to resist *that*!

"Okay," Ardith called, after about ten minutes. "I know you all must have worked hard last night, so we'll call practice short today. See you tomorrow."

Pres's eyebrows shot up. Man, the lady really was going soft this year! Call practice over early? What next?

Hope and Peter were the first to leave the gym.

Jessica picked up her pompon and walked past Pres. She smiled at him, but prepared to keep on going. Pres stopped her by springing to his feet and jumping down off the riser to land directly in front of her.

"Hey, you were good."

"Why, thanks." Jessica raised her sparkling green gaze to his.

"I mean, *really* good. You'll be a great addition to Varsity. Your moves are so smooth and — " he paused, gave her a sideways smile, and added — irresistible."

She laughed, tossing her brown hair behind her.

"Well, then I guess I'd better work on that. I

29

wouldn't want to distract the players from the game," she quipped.

Pres returned her laughter and she went out the door.

Olivia pushed past Pres without even saying hello. She'd heard him compliment Jessica and a shaft of pain seemed to be slicing through her heart. Now *Pres* had gone over to the other side! Where was his loyalty to the old squad? Had he forgotten them all, her included, so quickly? He used to think *she* was the outstanding one, and had even been a little in awe of her skills sometimes when she was particularly daring. And now it was as if she didn't exist anymore. It was Jessica, only Jessica, he saw.

I will control myself until I get home, she promised herself as she walked woodenly down the hall. I'll go into my room, I'll lock the door — even if it does drive my mother crazy — and then, and then I'll curl up in a little ball and sleep for about a hundred years.

Tara had spotted Pres just seconds after he'd come into the gym. A guy like that drew your attention instantly by his mere presence. She'd deliberately dawdled, making a show of tying her sneaker lace, so she'd be the last female to walk by him. Ever since he'd "rescued" her from that bar Sean had taken her to up at the lake, Pres had popped into her mind on several occasions. Snaring a guy on a permanent basis wasn't on Tara's list of top ten aspirations, but Pres intrigued her. Mostly because he was by far the handsomest guy she knew in town, and because he outclassed them all. Cultivating his interest would certainly be a coup for her.

She approached him now, her expression as provocative as she could make it.

Pres caught the look and smiled to himself. The flaming redhead was about to meet somebody who intended to turn up the heat. He took a stance directly in her path, legs apart, hands thrust into the front pockets of his jeans. He regarded her with a blantantly interested look.

"Well, hello again, stranger," Tara said in her attractive voice. She knew her voice was one of her best features, and she used it to her advantage. She came to a halt practically inches from Pres's chest and looked up at him from beneath her dark lashes, dark due to several coats of black mascara.

Pres gave a wide, slow grin. "Hi. You looked mighty good out there."

"You think so?" Tara raised her chin, staring directly into Pres's eyes. He stared straight back at her. She felt like a million dollars. Pres was really and truly looking *at* her, not through her. He looked at her as if she were the most important thing in the world to him. It felt so good to get all this direct, undiluted male attention.

"So, how do you like cheerleading? Is it as great as you'd hoped?"

"Yep. But it's also a lot harder than I expected. Sometimes I don't think I'll ever get the moves right." Tara's eyes concentrated on Pres's as if she were memorizing them.

Pres chuckled. "I don't think you'll have any

31

trouble with the moves at all. When you're out on the court or field, every guy's eyes will be directly on you," Pres predicted.

Tara smiled widely, thrilled by his words. "Do you care to put that down in writing? I wouldn't want to forget a line like that."

Pres laughed and said, "I'll do better than that. Let me walk you to the locker room and tell you a few more times so you'll have it memorized."

Sean Dubrow pretended to be balancing his megaphone on the tip of his middle finger. If Mrs. E. caught him, she'd have a fit, but he didn't care. He was using the activity to cover up the fact that he was really watching Pres flirt with Tara, and Tara make a play for Pres. Sean clenched his jaw and ground his teeth. He felt intense dislike building up inside, like steam in a confined space with no place to go. The last thing he wanted was for a guy from last year's Varsity Squad to come waltzing in here thinking he could poach on Sean's turf. Where did Pres get off trying to do that? This was Sean's territory, and he intended to defend it.

Pres had had his year in the limelight. But he was graduated now. This was *Sean's* year. This was *his* year to capture all the girl's fancies. And he especially had no intention of letting some guy who didn't belong on the high school scene anymore come in and take one of the Varsity girls. Being on the squad had been the first step Sean had taken so he could be in a position to pursue any girl he wanted — especially Varsity girls who were the most sought after by all the guys in school.

Sean watched Pres and Tara turn and proceed through the gym doors. He dropped the megaphone with a vicious-sounding clatter. Preston Tilford III was not going to come in here and take Tara. Not if Sean could help it. He'd show that jerk where to go and he'd get Tara for himself — no matter what it took to do it.

CHAPTER

Out of a fog Olivia heard her name.

"Olivia Evans! Olivia Evans!"

She blinked, her vision cleared, and Mr. Spencer's surly face came into focus. He stood at the front of the science room, glowering at her.

Olivia was fairly certain that Mr. Spencer hated getting up in the morning, hated coming to school, hated his job, and more than anything, hated teenagers. It was rumored around school that he was due to retire in two more years, and there were bets being made that he wouldn't even last that long.

Olivia hated being singled out by any teacher, but especially by Mr. Spencer. It meant a highly embarrassing verbal attack was about to be launched, and she wasn't even sure what she'd done to earn it.

"Do you read me now, Miss Evans?" Dark

gray bushy eyebrows frowned at her. "I thought you'd died in your seat and gone to cheerleader heaven from that glassy-eyed expression on your face," Mr. Spencer continued.

Olivia heard quiet laughter all around her, while she felt the blood creeping in a hot flush up her neck and face.

"I'm sorry," was all she could get out.

"No doubt," Mr. Spencer said tartly. "Now that I have your undivided attention, would you be so kind as to answer the question?" He regarded her through slitted eyes that reminded Olivia of a predator about to strike. She began to feel a panicky sensation twisting her stomach.

"What — what question?"

The gray brows rose and there was more giggling and smirking in the classroom.

"The question, Miss Evans? The *question* is number three from the homework I assigned *yesterday*, and which I just asked the class to pull out *today*," he answered with heavy emphasis.

It didn't do Olivia any good. She didn't have the homework assignment. She hadn't even heard it assigned. She'd been anesthetized or something yesterday. She'd just floated into class, found her seat by habit, sat there in a trance, and somehow had been conscious enough to hear the bell ending class. Certainly she'd never been aware that an assignment had been made.

The panic that had been rising inside her became a tidal wave that threatened to engulf her. She licked dry lips and tried to think of an excuse.

Mr. Spencer didn't wait for whatever lies

would spring from her lips. "No homework, Miss Evans? Charming. I assume waving your pompon after school is wearing you out so much you don't have time to do more important tasks." His eyes burned as he turned away abruptly, saying very distinctly to her, "Do tonight's homework, *last* night's homework, read the next two chapters in your book, and write a five-page synopsis of the material."

Olivia held back a gasp. The next two chapters plus a five-page synopsis?! But those chapters had to be fifteen pages apiece and boring enough to put even the most conscientious of kids to sleep.

She slumped back and tried to focus on her desk through watery eyes, knowing everyone was staring at her. She could almost bet what they were thinking: Olivia Evans, last year's Varsity Cheerleading Squad's best gymnastic performer, couldn't cut it this year. She didn't have what it took. She was a loser, no longer able to be the lead gymnast, and a has-been scholar, too. Poor Olivia, burned out at seventeen, a future of under-achievement staring her in the face.

The buzzer sounded, mercifully ending class, and Olivia rose and walked out of the science room by instinct.

She'd hoped to escape without comment from her classmates, but it had been a futile hope. Olivia hadn't gotten five feet down the hall before she heard, "Well, it looks like being a rah-rah girl isn't as easy as they say it is. I guess even a *cheerleader* can be a victim of the famous senior slump."

"Yes, and I heard Mrs. Engborg won't let you stay on the squad if you can't even maintain a B average in your classes," someone else added.

Olivia refused to turn around and acknowledge the sniping going on behind her back. It was from two girls who hadn't made Varsity. She knew they were deliberately trying to be mean and vindictive, so she acted as if she were in one of her trances and totally unaware of anything going on around her.

Doggedly she marched to her locker to change books for her next and last class for the day. A B average. That was ridiculously easy to maintain, and she'd always been a high B or A student. Those stupid girls were the ones who wouldn't have been able to hack it academically if they'd tried to combine cheerleading and school. She, Olivia, had no trouble with that!

She trailed the other students into math class where the teacher was handing back a pop quiz she'd given the day before. As Olivia sank into her seat, Mrs. Hawkins placed her paper on her desk. The look Mrs. Hawkins gave Olivia was one of puzzlement and concern, but she didn't say anything as she moved on down the row.

Olivia was about to simply cram her quiz paper into her notebook, when her glance touched disinterestedly on the grade at the top. Her mouth dropped open. A 59! How on earth had she managed to get that? Granted, math this year included calculus, and it was harder than ever before, but Olivia had been sure she would ace the quiz. Math had always been her easiest subject. But a 59? It was an F!

Before anyone else could see her grade, Olivia shoved the paper deep into her notebook. She'd look at it later to see what she'd done wrong. It was probably a simple case of making a few dumb mistakes in calculation.

Mrs. Hawkins was now at the front of the class, beginning to lecture, but Olivia tuned her out. Against her will she was remembering what those creepy girls had said. Senior slump. That was for kids who didn't care about school or grades anymore. And they got it in winter, not at the beginning of the school year. It certainly didn't apply to *her*. She had always strived to be superior in whatever she set out to do, whether it was school or cheerleading. But, a little nasty voice said, way deep down inside, You're not *the* best in one of those areas anymore, are you? Olivia felt something cave in inside her chest, as if a crushing weight were making it difficult to breathe.

With a superhuman will, Olivia ripped her attention away from these inner thoughts and tried to listen to the math lecture, but it wasn't easy, and forty minutes later when the period ended, she didn't have the slightest idea what Mrs. Hawkins had said. Well, it didn't matter, she told herself. She'd just borrow somebody's notes. Right now she had to get down to the locker room to change for cheerleading practice.

* * *

Jessica was doing some deep leg stretches with her usual grace when she saw Patrick Henley come in with Pres. He was looking fully as handsome as he had when he'd come up to the lake with Pres and Walt to watch the new squad practice. He really was a hunk, with a tall, strong body and that winning smile. When he smiled, Jessica realized it came to him often and with ease. He was a guy who always appeared happy and laughing about something. But that didn't detract in any way from his sheer physical impact.

Jessica wondered what had happened between Patrick and Mary Ellen Kirkwood, last year's Varsity captain. It was common knowledge that for Patrick Henley, there hadn't existed any females except for her — at least last year. But Mary Ellen had gone to New York City to become a model, leaving Patrick here in Tarenton.

Jessica watched Patrick recline on a riser beside Pres, her green eyes riveted on him. She felt an unfamiliar pull of attraction and admiration for such a great-looking male. Unlike Sean, Patrick was not consumed with his own good looks to the point where he practically swaggered and expected girls to fall in front of him like mown grass. Patrick actually seemed unaware that he was handsome.

Before Jessica could think much more about him, Mrs. Engborg walked into the gym, carrying her boom box. They were continuing to work on the cheer she'd devised from all of their routines. Jessica thought Mrs. Engborg had worked

39

up a spectacular edition. If they ever got it down right, it would have the fans in the stands screaming, and jumping up and down.

Ardith caught sight of Pres and Patrick out of the corner of her eye and smiled. She didn't have to strain herself to figure out what the big attraction was for those two. She just hoped the cheerleaders could ignore them and practice with the single-minded devotion Ardith demanded of them.

Ardith took a head count. "Where's Olivia?"

Tara waved her hand in the direction of the door. "She was just changing when I came up. She should be here by now."

Ardith pursed her lips. That girl had better get here pronto or she was going to have to take some disciplinary measures. Being late for practice was not something Ardith tolerated, and Olivia knew that.

Right then the door from the hall swung open and Olivia came in. She didn't have her usual bounce or the look of determination she'd had last year, but still, she did appear ready to work. Whatever was going on inside her head, she was still enough of a professional that she didn't let it affect her cheerleading, Ardith thought. Or at least not much.

"Hey, Livvy!" Patrick called, and Olivia's face brightened momentarily as she heard his deep voice. Then she noticed Pres sitting beside him and her expression became blank.

"Hi, Patrick. No garbage awaits today?"

"Garbage *always* awaits. But I don't think anybody will steal it before I get there, do you?" Patrick teased with his quirky grin.

That grin was so familiar it brought a rush of memories flooding back into Olivia's mind and she felt an incredible yearning for last year's squad members. Much as she liked seeing Patrick's smiling face, maybe it wasn't such a good idea that he was here. She hoped he wouldn't come around often.

"No, I guess not," she answered, and walked over to the other five cheerleaders.

Mrs. Engborg appeared to be exerting herself to be patient. "Okay, now that we're all here, let's get going. Take your places." She turned on the music she'd taped to help them keep in step and move together while they learned the routine, and the six started in.

Patrick watched the cheerleaders, and then found his attention constantly coming back to one girl, the beautiful brown-haired one with the sparkling green eyes. Man, was Jessica something! Long legs. Beautiful legs. Graceful legs. Patrick was a sucker for great legs. Of course, the fact that they were attached to a pretty superlooking girl didn't exactly hurt. Jessica Bennett. He hadn't really noticed her last year. Their worlds just hadn't touched. Not that he would have noticed her anyway, not as long as Mary Ellen was on the scene.

Patrick frowned. Mary Ellen. Good old Melon hadn't written more than two postcards since she'd hightailed it to the big city. She'd said she was involved in dance classes, auditions, and photography sessions to upgrade her portfolio. She had too little time and too much activity to keep in touch. But Patrick figured if she had even a shred of feeling left for him, she'd have *made* the time to write.

Patrick's gaze fell on Jessica again. Man, she was good at what she did! The way she moved, it was as if she thumbed her nose at gravity. Narrow hips, slim waist, long legs, graceful arms — Patrick stopped the inventory with a grin. He was certainly getting excited over her.

The knowledge that he was actually capable of being attracted to another girl like this surprised him. What should he do about it? If he asked Jessica for a date, would she accept? A knockout like that must have more offers than she could handle, but he'd give it a whirl. The worst she could do was turn him down. Patrick could deal with that. Mary Ellen had gotten him really used to rejection. He'd just go run through his garbage route in record time and then buzz back here at six and wait for her outside the school.

He touched Pres on the arm. "Gotta shove off, buddy, I feel the irresistible urge to empty cans and commune with trash."

Pres nodded and looked back out on the floor. "Right. See you."

Patrick smiled to himself as he loped out through the doors to the hall. He didn't need a crystal ball to know Pres was getting interested in that redhead. That was just fine with Patrick. It left the field more open for him to try to zero in on Jessica. If she was even vaguely interested in a *garbage* man, unlike certain other females.

When he'd visited the new Varsity Squad up at the lake and talked to Jessica around the camp fire, she'd certainly listened courteously enough as he'd explained about his garbage and moving businesses. But it was one thing to talk to a guy about hauling trash; it was quite another thing to date him and have to ride in his truck.

CHAPTER

Patrick actually thought twice about whether he ought to exchange his garbage truck for the moving van he and Pres owned before he went back to the school to see Jessica. Since Pres had his Porsche he didn't need the van, and sometimes Patrick used it. He'd done that a few times when Mary Ellen had been around, since Patrick had been painfully aware of her attitude about being seen in a garbage truck.

But he finally decided that if he were going to date any girl, it would be on *his* terms. If she was turned off by his method of transportation, then he'd forget about her.

Almost defiantly he drove the garbage truck into the Tarenton High parking lot. One consideration he did make was to shed his white coveralls before hopping out and walking up the front steps. It was six-ten, and he figured the girls were probably still blowing their hair dry, and that he hadn't missed Jessica.

He hung around the massive lobby, hardly seeing the familiar, huge trophy case, the vast oil painting, or the large metal sculpture. Years of seeing those things had made them so familiar he didn't notice them anymore.

He paced across the wide marble floor like a nervous lion, and was startled when Pres shoved away from the wall and said, "Well, well, what are you doing back here?" He grinned as if he knew full well why Patrick had returned.

"Uh — I — " Patrick suddenly felt at a loss for words, and then was grateful when the arrival of the girls saved him.

The girls' voices reached Patrick and Pres as they came down the hall from the stairwell leading from the floor below, where the locker rooms were.

"I think it's got a lot of potential," Jessica was saying. "By the time we've got it perfected, it'll be a guaranteed crowd-pleaser. Don't you think so, Hope?"

Hope Chang smiled at Jessica. She really liked Jessica and appreciated her attempt to include her in the conversation she'd been having with Tara.

"Yes, I do," she agreed, making her medium length, straight dark hair bounce. "The way Mrs. Engborg brought together all those moves from our different cheers shows why she's been cheerleading coach for so many years."

"Right," Jessica said heartily, and beamed at

Hope, her lovely green eyes warm and friendly. Then she noticed Patrick standing off to the side of the hall.

At that precise moment, Pres walked up to Tara. Sean and Peter came up the stairs in back of them.

Pres regarded Tara as if he owned her and said, "Need a lift?"

"Sure do," she replied, looking extremely pleased with the situation.

Pres and Tara walked out the front door together, leaving Hope and Jessica standing there. Hope had slowed her pace and was gazing sideways at Peter, watching him approach from behind.

Quick to see the interest in Hope's expression, Jessica left her side and went over to Patrick. If Hope was alone, Peter would stop to talk to her, Jessica knew.

She smiled at Patrick. "Back again? Didn't lose something, did you?"

Patrick smiled back at her, feeling an immense pull of attraction for this beautiful, willowy girl. "Yeah, in fact I did. I lost the opportunity to ask you out." He smiled even wider, appearing from the outside to be a supremely confident male, but inwardly feeling vague anxiety at the possibility of Jessica's refusal.

"Ohhhh?" Jessica drawled in a lilting voice. She cocked her head to the side, then made an elaborate examination of the floor around them. Bending down, she picked up something imaginary and pretended to hand it to Patrick.

46

He put out his hand, palm up, amusement on his face. "What's this?"

"Your lost opportunity. Looks like I just found it," Jessica answered Patrick, as laughter creased his face.

"Ah," he said, eyebrows raised in understanding. He tucked the "lost-and-found" article in his pocket and asked, "So how'd you like to go to the movies this Friday?" In spite of Jessica's warm, encouraging smile, he still felt a certain amount of apprehension. How many times had Mary Ellen given out positive vibes, only to turn around and symbolically slap him in the face by changing her mind?

"I'd love to," Jessica said with warmth and genuine enthusiasm.

Patrick was temporarily stunned, but he managed to cover up that feeling and say, "Great. Tell me where you live and I'll be there at seven Friday."

Jessica turned and walked toward the front door, saying teasingly, "Well, if you'd give me a lift home right now I could *show* you where I live."

Patrick felt momentary astonishment at this sudden success, but he leapt at the chance to take her home. "Sure thing," he said eagerly, stepping forward to escort her out the door. Then his steps faltered. Was she aware he drove a garbage truck? How should he explain it? Apologetically? Or not at all?

Finally he opted for the approach that had always been natural to him. They walked through the front doors and out into the early evening air, where the huge garbage truck stood in the parking lot as if someone had placed it there as a joke.

"My steed awaits," Patrick said with an elaborate flourish of his hand. He regarded her with a sideways glance, but Jessica didn't bat an eye.

"A garbage truck! How original. I bet no one runs *you* off the road." She laughed and walked over to the passenger side door, as Patrick ran to open it for her.

He felt a rather unfamiliar emotion. He hadn't identified it until the two of them were settled in the truck and he'd started the engine. It was gratitude. Intense gratitude that Jessica Bennett had enough class to make the best of any situation — even being taken home by a garbage man in his truck.

Hope smiled shyly as Peter Rayman came closer. Peter caught the smile and returned it. There was something about her sweet face that really appealed to him. Not to mention her quiet, thoughtful personality. Peter hadn't had much exposure to Asians, and of course Hope and her family were fully as American as he was, but still, you couldn't look at her face and forget her origins. He really liked that.

He walked up to her, ignoring Sean, and said, "Practice went well today, didn't it? I think I can begin to see us actually looking good at this Saturday's game."

"Yeah," Hope agreed. "It'll be our first game of the year. The first time we do our stuff in front of the whole school. I guess I'd be lying if I said I wasn't a little nervous. How about you?"

Peter came to stand beside her, noting that Jessica had gone off with that big guy, Patrick Henley, that Tara and Pres had left together, and that Sean was standing out on the front steps staring after them.

"A little," he admitted, knowing Sean couldn't hear him make this admission. If Sean had been within hearing distance, the urge to lie would have been strong. And he didn't want to have to lie to Hope — ever. "Got a ride home?"

"Well, I was going to catch the bus. . . ."

"Don't do that. I'll drop you off." Peter's mother had been sick and hadn't gone to work today so he had her Toyota. He didn't know when he'd get another chance to offer Hope — or any girl — a ride in such a nice car, so he wasn't going to miss this one.

Hope's face lit up with a smile. "That would be great. I'm not too crazy about the bus."

The two of them walked companionably out the door, side by side. Hope felt her heart skip a beat. Since the fire at the cabin, more and more she was beginning to think of Peter Rayman as a very special guy.

CHAPTER

7

Sean Dubrow was not the type of guy to take any kind of setback lying down. Before practice today he'd been prepared to ask Tara out. He'd show her a time so great, she wouldn't *want* to date any other guy. He'd carefully laid the ground work by giving her interested looks throughout practice. He'd been lifting up Jessica or Olivia, but he'd had eyes only for Tara. To a degree she'd responded, but he'd felt sure her first interest had been captured by Pres, lounging on the risers.

It infuriated Sean. Didn't that guy have anything better to do than hang around a high school from which he'd graduated, ogling the cheerleaders? Didn't he work or something? Sean knew Pres had refused to work for his family's company, Tarenton Fabricators, defying his father's wishes. Preston Tilford II was a man to be reckoned with, according to Sean's dad, a top salesman for the company. How Pres had had the temerity to thumb his nose at his dad, Sean couldn't guess, and in a way he gave him grudging admiration for it.

But Sean wished Pres had gone off to Princeton like his father wanted him to. Then he'd be off the scene, leaving the field open for Sean. Sean liked competition, but he hated failure, and in his opinion, Tara's choosing to ride home with Pres was a defeat.

But not for long, Sean thought determinedly. Only temporarily. The setback merely heightened Sean's need to excel, to win, to conquer. And conquer he would.

He'd start with a well-worded phone call tonight. . . .

"So how's the business going?" Jessica asked, sitting upright, taking in the new feeling of gazing at the world from a higher vantage point.

Patrick glanced at her as he turned out of the parking lot. "Which one?"

"Both, for that matter. But specifically the moving business. I hear it's really getting off the ground now." She aimed her green gaze at him, inquiringly.

A guy could get lost in those gorgeous emerald eyes, Patrick thought fleetingly, before he ripped his attention back to the road. "How'd you know that?"

"Oh, come on. Everybody in school knows about the famous H and T's TLC Moving," Jessica explained about Patrick and Pres's business

51

venture, as if it were nothing extraordinary. She smiled widely at him.

Patrick felt corded muscles in his neck ease up, as if they'd been tensed for a barbed remark.

"Business is going okay," he said with a careless shrug. "We seem to be finally developing a good reputation, and Pres has been drumming up a lot of business, what with all of his family's contacts. We're actually moving more things now than we're breaking," he said, laughing.

"That's good," Jessica laughed and rolled her eyes. She slanted her body in the seat to look at Patrick more directly. She admired any young man who seemed to have his act together; someone who had two businesses was obviously a gogetter, someone with the potential to be a real success in life. "Got any plans for expansion in the future?" she asked.

Patrick looked at her and shrugged. "I've always got ideas about expansion. As for plans, well. . . ." He talked and told her his dreams, and the time it took to drive her home shrank to nothing.

As he watched her bounce up the walkway to her house, he was glad Friday night was only two nights away.

Tara was reluctant to leave the rich confines of the red Porsche. Pres didn't seem to be in an awfully big hurry to see her go, either. But they'd been parked in her driveway talking for fully fifteen minutes now, and she was sure she'd seen

52

the curtains over the living room window move twice. Not that whoever was in there would really care that much about why she and Pres were sitting out there all this time. But still, Tara supposed she ought to be making getting-out-of-the-car moves.

She gripped the handle of the door, saying, "Well, thanks for the ride. It sure beats calling my mom and having her break up something to come get me."

"Break up something?" Pres asked, teasing. "Like what?

Tara laughed, throwing her head back to reveal the beautiful creamy skin on her neck.

Pres couldn't help noticing what great skin she had. But he didn't know that showing it off was a deliberate move on her part.

"Well, I was referring to a bridge game, actually," Tara said, then gave Pres a stunning parting smile that said, *Ask me out.*

But he didn't. He just smiled back a slow, suggestive smile. The kind of smile some guys had who seemed to be so sure of a girl, they knew they wouldn't have to work at getting her. They knew all they'd have to do would be call her up at a moment's notice and she'd leap at the chance to go out with them.

Tara didn't like that. She wanted to be the kind of girl guys were *never* sure of, the kind guys were always anxious about. She wanted to be *in* control, not controlled.

She thrust open the door and headed up the

walk, deliberately making the view Pres got of her retreating body so provocative he'd be sorry he hadn't asked her out.

Oddly, he was. He even toyed with the idea of running up the steps and catching her before she got inside, but then he got a hold of himself in time. A phone call later would be adequate. Pres was not some inexperienced boy to be dangled by a girl. He was a man of the world, graduated, and a business entrepreneur. *He* would be in command. *He* would call the shots.

Tara turned and wiggled her fingers at him in farewell before she stepped inside. Right, I'm in control, Pres thought. Just until I can get home and dial her number. Chuckling, he backed the Porsche out of the drive.

Olivia sat on the edge of her bed, staring at her image in the bureau mirror against the wall. When she'd come home after practice, her mother had looked up from the meal she was preparing, then had done a double take. Almost immediately she'd dropped what she was doing and rushed over to her daughter, demanding, "What's wrong? Are you sick?"

Olivia had ducked the hand that had shot out to feel her forehead to take her temperature.

"*Moth*-er, I'm fine. Just a little — " she'd hesitated to say it, but couldn't think of anything else in the split second she'd had " — tired. But I'll be fine after a nap."

With a lot of protests and arguments her mother had allowed her to retreat to her room, where she now sat, staring at herself. What had made her mother think she wasn't feeling well? Did she really look it?

And why did she feel genuinely tired? Last year after every practice, she had felt tired, but it had been different from the way she felt right now. Last year she had felt the physically exhausted but mentally exhilarated tiredness that came from proving herself. Now she felt a bone-weary, mental tiredness that seemed to be taking over her body, eating away at it, leaving an empty feeling behind. Why?

Suddenly it was all just too much for Olivia. She really didn't care why she felt the way she did.

She glanced at the clock, knew her mother would be calling her any moment for dinner, and lay back down on the bed.

When her mother's voice sounded down the hall, Olivia didn't hear her. She was sound asleep.

CHAPTER

8

Tara was sitting at her desk when the pale pink Princess phone beside her bed started ringing. She leapt at it, hoping it was Samantha Gray, to whom she could recount being taken home by Preston Tilford III.

Surprise registered on Tara's face as she heard Sean Dubrow identify himself and say, "I just called to say I think you really looked great out there at practice today. Maybe Olivia and Jessica have all the spectacular moves, but you've really got your act together."

Tara smiled and lay back against the three pillows on her bed, two encased in pink and green flowered ruffled shams. "Really?" she asked, feeling pleasure course through her. She remembered how Sean had appeared to be watching her throughout practice. She knew he wouldn't have done that unless he'd been impressed.

56

"Really. In fact, it seems to me that when you cheer at Saturday's game all the guys in the stands are going to have trouble keeping their eyes off you." Sean was lying back on his bed, imagining the response his compliment was achieving at the other end of the line. "And I'm not so sure I like that," he added insinuatingly.

"What?" Tara sat bolt upright. What did he mean by that? That he didn't like the idea that she'd be stealing the show from the other girls?

"You heard me. All those guys staring at you, watching your every move in that cute short skirt. No, I don't think I like that. A guy never likes it if other guys are staring at a girl he's interested in. Makes them have ideas he doesn't like. . . ." He stopped suggestively and waited for her to take the bait.

She bit.

"Ohhhh. Well, what can I say?" she countered in a teasing voice.

"You could say you'll take pity on a lonesome guy and go out with me next Friday night."

Tara smiled to herself, envisioning someone like Sean lonesome. Only if the end of the world came Thursday. But still. . . . Then she frowned slightly. She'd hoped Pres would ask her out for Friday night, but he hadn't. She wondered why. Because he wasn't interested in her enough? She didn't think that was it. Maybe he had other commitments that didn't leave him free that night. Whatever the reason, Sean was waiting for an answer. Sean *was* a hunk, the guy who really turned heads in school. Tara would be the object

57

of a lot of admiration if she was seen out with him.

"Sure, why not?" she said finally, allowing enough time to elapse between his question and her answer so Sean wouldn't think she'd been waiting for this invitation. Keep a guy on his toes, that was her motto.

"Good," Sean said evenly, exultant over this small triumph. "I'll pick you up about seven."

"Where are we going?"

"Now, if I told you that, it would ruin the surprise," Sean said with a smile in his voice.

"Oh, well, I sure wouldn't want that," Tara laughed, but at the same time she was piqued that Sean wasn't telling her where they were going. How was she supposed to dress? Fancy or funky? Well she'd dress the way she wanted and if it didn't suit him, or the place they went, so what?

"Great. I'll see you at practice tomorrow," Sean said and they hung up. He lay on his back, staring up at the ceiling for a long time after that, plotting.

Tara got up from her bed and walked over to her desk. She'd gone out with her share of boys in the past, but they'd always told her where they were going beforehand. She wasn't sure she liked this. Not knowing where they'd be going meant she didn't have control over the situation, made her feel slightly off balance. She'd have to be ready for anything. She could do it, sure, but she preferred being forewarned.

Her thoughts were interrupted when the phone

beside her bed rang again. It had to be Samantha this time.

But it wasn't.

Tara's eyes widened when Pres Tilford said, "Hi, there. I forgot to ask you something today." He kept his tone totally casual, as if he hadn't been waiting for the proper amount of time to elapse since they'd last been together before calling her.

"What?" Just for a moment Tara felt panic, but she trampled it down.

"I forgot to tell you where I was taking you Friday night," Pres announced as he waited for the sound of delight he expected to hear in Tara's voice.

Instead there was a brief pause, followed by Tara asking in an odd-sounding voice, "Oh? Where?"

Ardith studied her cheerleaders and decided practicing on a Friday night was the worst of all. She could tell they were like coiled springs. Whether it was because this was their last chance to practice before their first game tomorrow, or because it was Friday night, the night teenagers seemed to think had been invented for the express purpose of partying, she didn't know. She just wished she could issue an edict forbidding them any kind of social life the night before a game.

I'm like a mother hen, she thought, wanting to shoo my chicks back into the nest.

She sighed and blew her whistle. "Break!"

Hope sank down on the bottom riser and contemplated making out her will. Ardith was like a slave driver tonight, pushing them to excel, wanting them to be the best they could be. But she's killing us in the process, Hope thought, studying her fellow cheerleaders for evidence of their imminent expiration.

Tendrils of Tara's lovely red hair were plastered to the sides of her damp face, and she looked like she was taking her last breath.

Tara felt breathless all right, but it wasn't due to exertion. It was nerves. Pres Tilford had just sauntered into the gym, and she knew he expected to be taking her out tonight.

But so did Sean.

I could kill myself for getting into this mess, Tara thought momentarily. She did want to go out with Sean, but she wanted to know where they were going. Tara hadn't said anything to Sean at last night's practice about their destination, and neither had he spoken to her. But Pres, on the other hand, *had* told her where he was taking her — to dinner at a posh place in neighboring Garrison. She'd been there a couple of times and liked it fine, but of course the real attraction was Pres himself.

Out of the corner of her eye she saw Sean approaching, and she knew he was utilizing the break in practice to make his move. What was she going to do?

"Hey, gorgeous. All ready for tonight?" Sean stood in front of her, completely blocking her view of Pres. Whether deliberately or accidentally, Tara didn't know, but she was glad. If she couldn't see Pres, he couldn't see her.

"What?" She feigned ignorance and looked at Sean questioningly.

He frowned and crossed his arms in front of his muscular chest.

"Don't tell me you forgot? We're going out tonight." He regarded her through narrowed eyes. What was she pulling?

Tara's eyes flew open wider and she gasped, collecting her thoughts. Talk about good acting! Save me an Oscar, she thought. "Tonight? You mean you were asking me out for *tonight*?"

"I said *Friday*," Sean answered tersely, the muscles in his jaw tightening.

Tara poured on the charm. Lightly she laid a hand on his arm in a conciliatory gesture. "Oh, Sean, I'm so *sorry*. You mean you weren't asking me out for *next* Friday night? You said *next* Friday, not *this* Friday." She raised her hands in a helpless gesture, accompanied by an appropriately contrite expression.

Sean didn't remember what he'd said exactly. But it didn't make any difference. "Just a matter of wording," Sean waved aside this argument. "I've already make reservations for tonight at Chez Marcel. Then I thought we'd hit that club in Garrison afterward for a little cheek-to-cheek." Sean moved closer as if he were going to whisk her into his arms for some dancing right there in the gym. He decided she really had thought he'd meant next week, but that was okay. "The reservations aren't until eight. You'll have plenty of time to get home and change into your dancing shoes." He grinned confidently, ready for her to capitulate. Girls always did.

"I can't."

"What?"

"I — ah — well, I can't go out tonight! Sorry. I already have plans for *this* Friday. But I'm free *next* Friday. The guy I thought was taking me out then, isn't." The joke wasn't funny and neither of them laughed.

Sean went to open his mouth, but whatever he was going to say got drowned out by a blast from Ardith's whistle.

"Okay, back into position. Five minutes are up. Let's go." She clapped her hands and the other four cheerleaders lined up, with obvious gaps in the line where Sean and Tara belonged.

"Ahem! Could we be so rude as to break into your little tête à tête over there for some work?" Ardith looked at Tara and Sean. As far as she was concerned, the two were simply engaged in a little flirting. She wasn't against it, but she wished they'd do it on their own time.

"Talk to you after practice," Tara said with a smile, and ran lightly over to take her place.

Chez Marcel! That was even a cut above the place Pres was taking her. And afterward Pres had planned on just bringing her home. He'd said she needed her rest before their first game tomorrow. But *she* wanted to party. She was young, not ready for an old person's bedtime. She bet when

Pres was a cheerleader, he didn't "rest" before a game.

Sean wanted to give her a great time. She had to convince him to give her a rain check, before he found out she was going out with Pres, and that Pres had spoken to her *after* she'd spoken to Sean. Or should she cancel out on Pres and go with Sean instead?

It was a tough decision. Chez Marcel, dancing, and Sean, versus dinner with Pres and a nine o'clock bedtime. Maybe she could convince Pres to take her out dancing just a *little* bit. She'd have to get to Pres right after practice and see if he would change his mind before she talked to Sean.

CHAPTER

Hope Chang resisted the desire to do cartwheels into the girls' locker room. Peter had just asked her if she wanted to go to a movie tonight! If they handed out awards for saying the word *yes* in three seconds or less, she'd have won. It was the first time he'd really asked for a date.

The door swung shut behind her and she actually did perform one perfect cartwheel down the line of lockers. If she'd been cheering at a game it would have earned her some really enthusiastic applause, there was so much snap and vitality to it. She landed smartly on her feet and zipped over to her locker, whirling the combination lock dial. She was so excited for a second there she even forgot her combination!

Jessica looked at her sideways and said, "Hey, somebody! You can turn out the lights. Hope's bright enough to light up the locker room all by herself."

Hope broke into a big smile and turned to face Jessica.

"Let me guess. You won the lottery," Jessica said facetiously.

Hope shook her head, smiling even more.

"No? Well, then, let's see. Ah! I have it. The principal just told you you're so smart you don't have to do your senior year, that you can graduate in June without it!"

"Nope, Mrs. Oetjen would never say that." Hope laughed with a hair-swinging shake. Her hair was like black silk, Jessica thought. And even after shaking it vigorously, it fell into place. Oh, to have hair like that! Every morning Jessica had to energetically attack hers with an entire beautician's arsenal: styling mousse, hair dryer, and curling iron.

"I give up." She started to turn away, then said dramatically, "Oh! It can't be that Peter Rayman was just talking to you and asked you out for pizza and a movie, can it?" Jessica laughed when Hope ran over to her and gave her a hug, and she hugged Hope back. Goodness! Did love do this to a person?

"Yes, yes, and yes!" Hope sang, bouncing back to open her locker and drag out her towel. "I was beginning to give up. I thought for sure he'd ask me out when we got back from the lake, and when he didn't, I even thought he might be a little bit prejudiced."

"Peter? Never!" Jessica stated adamantly. "He probably doesn't even notice. I bet if you were to waltz right up to him and say, 'I'm Asian,' he'd say, 'You are!? I never noticed.' "

Hope laughed skeptically. "Oh, yeah. I'll bet."

"Really. Peter's about the least prejudiced person I know," Jessica insisted. "Go get him!"

"I am. I am. Can't you tell?" Hope smiled over her shoulder and started for the showers.

"No," Jessica called after her, "and you have to try harder with Peter. I think he's a little dense."

Hope laughed again and went into the shower.

Tara had come into the locker room just in time to catch the conversation between Jessica and Hope. She walked over to her locker, which was only three away from Jessica's.

"So Hope's going out, I'm going out. It's a shame you don't have a date tonight to sort of take your mind off the big game tomorrow." She smiled sympathetically at Jessica.

"Oh, but I do. I'm going to the movies with Patrick Henley."

"Oh? But, um, I heard he was really gone on Mary Ellen Kirkwood. You know, the captain of Varsity last year?" Tara said, surprised.

Jessica shrugged and wrapped her towel sarong fashion around her in preparation for hitting the showers. "He's probably bored. After all, she's in New York. I'm just someone to do something with for one night."

"Oh, that's too bad," Tara commiserated. "I guess a big romance would be out of the question with him carrying the torch for Mary Ellen."

Jessica regarded Tara's seemingly innocent expression for a moment and then stated flatly, "I'm not interested in a big romance. I like playing the field. Who needs to date just one guy when there are so many terrific ones out there?"

"Right on!" Tara endorsed, thinking back to the scene in the gym between herself and Sean and Pres. She had a date tonight with Pres as planned, but with his promise for a "short" trip to a club in the next town over, *and* a really great date planned with Sean for next week. Two guys, two dates. It was like winning both the gold and the silver medals.

Humming to herself, she followed Jessica into the shower room, meeting Hope just coming back.

Olivia, whose locker was one row over and out of sight from the others, stood staring into the darkness inside her locker. She thought about what Jessica had said about Patrick. Was it true? Did Patrick only have in mind passing some time with Jessica since Mary Ellen was away? Or was he planning something else? Could he have finally decided that Mary Ellen was gone, that she'd *never* be his, and it was time to find a replacement? And did he think that replacement would be Jessica? If he did, he was in for disappointment. If Patrick had his sights set on her, Olivia was afraid he was headed for more heartbreak. Jessica was a moving target.

Hope, Jessica, and Olivia left the locker room about the same time, with Tara delaying over her hair. With a big evening ahead, she wanted it perfect.

The three girls started up the stairs to the main floor. It was strangely dark and lonely in the halls, and it made Olivia feel gloomy.

"How do you think we'll do tomorrow, Olivia?" Hope asked, looking back at Olivia who was climbing the stairs as if each step brought her closer to doom.

Olivia was slow to answer, then she said, "Well, I suppose we'll do all right. Luckily the other team's cheerleaders are real duds. Last year at our first game we'd had a couple of extra practice sessions though, so we were ready. But I suppose the students won't really expect as much this year from Varsity, what with Mary Ellen, Angie, and the whole old squad gone."

Hope felt stung. She even felt her face grow warm at the implied criticism in Olivia's comment. She'd never really gotten to know Olivia, since Olivia had been a junior last year while she had been a sophomore.

There always seemed to be an unstated rule that there wasn't a lot of intermingling with people who weren't in your same class in school. Sort of a caste system, with each class being on a higher stratum than the one below it, starting with the seniors. This year, when she'd realized she was the only junior on the squad, she'd hoped she could turn to Olivia, who'd seemed to blend in with the five seniors on last year's squad so well, for advice. Now it looked like Olivia was a stuck-up senior herself. Tara made Hope feel uncomfortable and outclassed. Sean hardly looked at her now. The only ones she felt really comfortable with were Jessica, and, of course, Peter.

Hope brightened. And Peter had said he'd walk her to the bus stop and then pick her up later for the movie and pizza afterwards. Now there was a prospect to help her forget Olivia's thoughtless remark!

Jessica said staunchly, "I think we'll be terrific!"

Hope thought she made the statement a little too vehemently, as if she were trying to convince herself as well. But Olivia didn't seem to hear Jessica's comment.

Olivia turned at the top of the stairs to head out through the lobby. She was unaware of the troubled look Hope gave her, or of the annoyed one on Jessica's face. All she wanted to do was get home as quickly as possible so she could take a nap.

Unfortunately first she had to endure the trial of dinner with her parents. But she knew if she emphasized the need to get plenty of rest before the game tomorrow, she'd get no argument from her mother, and she'd have an interference-free evening once she was in the sanctuary of her room. If there was one thing her mother loved, it was for Olivia to be sensible and practically bedridden. If her mother had had her way, Olivia would have been a bubble child. And now *I'm* the one who'd like to be in a bubble, Olivia thought with a pang.

She walked out through the front doors and right into Pres. Pres — the traitor. His arms came around her to steady her and she flinched.

"That glad to see me?" Pres quipped.

"Sorry." Olivia stepped back. Pres frowned and was about to say something when Tara spoke up. She'd just come through the doors herself.

"I thought you were taking *me* out tonight." She smiled widely to hide the annoyance she'd felt at finding Pres's arms around Olivia. Had there been a romance between them last year she hadn't known about? That seemed about as likely as her falling for the Abominable Snowman.

"You don't expect to have me all to yourself, do you?" Pres deliberately baited her, liking the expression this brought to her face. She wasn't that sure of him. That was fine with him. Pres had the feeling that with a girl like Tara, you were never that sure yourself of how she was thinking or what she'd do. And Pres liked the odds to be either in his favor, or at the very least, even.

"As long as you don't expect the same," Tara returned saucily. She linked her arm in Pres's and said, "See you tomorrow," to the other cheerleaders who were grouped on the stone front steps, and the two headed for Pres's Porsche.

Peter came up behind Hope and said, "Ready to go?" She jumped. "Oh! I didn't know you were there! You surprised me."

"The night'll be full of surprises," Peter said. He was feeling oddly exuberant and realized it was partly due to getting away from his mother for the evening, and partly due to the prospect of being with Hope for their first official date. Would there be more after tonight? He intended to make sure of it.

70

Hope laughed softly and hugged her books to her chest with her right hand. She loved it when Peter seemed to be in a good mood; he could be a lot of fun.

The two of them walked side by side down the steps and suddenly Hope felt Peter's hand brush hers, tentatively, as if testing the waters. She brushed his hand back as if saying, "Come on, the water's fine." He took her hand in his, engulfing it and yet holding it gently, as if he were afraid he might crush it. Hope smiled up at him. It was going to be a wonderful night!

CHAPTER

Jessica stood in front of the mirror, assessing her looks. Did she look too funky? Would her stepfather freak out when she went downstairs in this? She could hear him now: "You look like you're going on a stake-out with Sonny Crockett. What is this, *Miami Vice*?"

Maybe she did. She decided to change from the pink tank top into a soft crepe camp shirt in pale yellow, but she'd keep the white blazer with the sleeves pushed up. Now, was the miniskirt still a bit too much?

Jessica sighed. She hated having to dress for dates with only one thought in mind: Would Daniel let her out of the house or would he have a fit? Not whether the boy would like it or not. Experience had taught her that boys seldom even noticed what you had on unless it was really outlandish or extremely sexy.

She sighed and took off the miniskirt, replacing it with a pair of crayon-green jeans. Conservative but safe, and guaranteed to get her out of the house without incident.

She heard the door bell ring. Patrick. What a nice guy. She couldn't think of too many guys of his caliber, and she decided it would really be fun to go out with him.

The noise in the Pizza Palace was practically deafening. Hope, squashed in a corner next to Peter, laughed across the table at Patrick Henley. He and Jessica had gone to the same movie as Hope and Peter, and when they'd found out they were all headed for the same place afterward, decided to hook up. Booths were at a premium. You had to get there before the rest of the movie mob and stake your claim.

Being with Patrick, Jessica, and Peter seemed like heaven to Hope. Here she was surrounded — literally — by people her age, and music. Some of the tunes coming from the jukebox would not have been her first choice, but still, she was happy to be in a place full of noise, energy, and youth. At home things were usually low-key and at times Hope craved something more lively.

"So, how many kisses did you count in that first row in the movie?" Peter asked.

"What kisses in the first row?" Jessica asked, wide-eyed. "Weren't we supposed to be watching the movie?"

Everyone laughed.

Then Patrick casually put his arm around Jessica, and asked, "What movie? I thought we were there for something else."

Jessica's brown hair fell around her face as she playfully punched him in the ribs.

Hope actually blushed. She and Peter had sat three rows behind Patrick and Jessica, and she had seen Patrick lean over and kiss Jessica's cheek once. How had they established such an easy and familiar relationship so fast? She and Peter had sat like brother and sister. She wasn't sure if it was because Peter was shy, or if he just wasn't that interested in her. Although if that were the case, why had he bothered to ask her out?

Someone slid by their booth balancing Cokes, spotted the Varsity members, and said, "Hey! Lots of luck on your debut at tomorrow's game. We'll cream them!"

"Thanks," they chorused.

Jessica, her brow wrinkled in thought, looked at Hope and Peter. "I wonder what Olivia is doing tonight?" she mused.

Olivia was having one of her arguments with her mother. She wondered if she could apply for an entry in the *Guinness Book of Records* for the most number of spats one could have with a parent.

"It's unnatural for a person to need all the rest you seem to need this year." Olivia recognized that line of argument for what it was and said nothing, biding her time.

Her mother continued. "Last year when you

74

were a cheerleader, you were more energetic. Too energetic. I could never get you to go to bed at a normal hour." Normal in whose opinion? Olivia wanted to ask. "Now you're always in your room." Mrs. Evans stood over her daughter and shook a finger at her. From Olivia's vantage point on the couch, her mother almost eclipsed the room. People who knew Mrs. Evans were continually perplexed at how she could have produced such a slim, lithe, tiny daughter.

Olivia was perplexed about something bigger — her whole life. In a kind of trance, she stared up at her mother, seeing her through a fog, and watched her shake her plump finger. She seemed to double in size every second. All Olivia wanted was to go to her room. Instead she was forced to sit here and listen to this ridiculous monologue about *Teenage Girls, The Normal Health Of*.

A spark of the old spunk ignited and Olivia decided she didn't have to sit here and take this like a small, naughty child. She stood, forcing her mother to step back in surprise.

"Mother, I have homework. If I don't get it done, my grades will drop. You want me to do my best in school, but I can't if I don't study."

Her mother's mouth opened and closed. Then she sputtered, "But you just said you were going to bed."

"I forgot I had a math test to study for. Calculus requires a lot of extra work."

Olivia walked out of the room and headed for her bedroom with as much dignity as she could muster. She really wanted to run down the hall, screaming, "Just leave me alone! Everyone else does!" *Like Walt.* Walt, who had abandoned her for college, and all the romantic opportunities he might find there.

She closed the door very, very, quietly, because it was the exact opposite from what she felt like doing, as though by controlling the urge she could prove to herself that she could still exert her iron will. But she had begun to doubt that lately.

She sank down on her bed and her gaze rested on her cheerleading uniform laid out ready for tomorrow. Their first game of the season. She remembered back a year ago to her first game ever. Mary Ellen was captain, and confident that she would be able to hold the spectators in the palm of her hand. Angie, the one-year veteran, full of nerves. Nancy, claiming she was so excited she felt like throwing up. Walt clowning around, trying to ease the tension. And Pres — cool as a polar ice cap.

What had her feelings been? Horrified, Olivia realized she couldn't remember. Images of the rest of the old Varsity Squad at that game lived in her mind as clearly as if she'd just seen them an hour ago. But her spot was totally blank, as if she'd never existed. Panicking, Olivia thought furiously, trying to force her stubborn mind to yield even an indistinct image of herself.

But it wouldn't.

What *had* she felt like then?

What did she feel like *now*? She was facing a brand-new squad tomorrow at their very first game. She knew they expected her, as captain, to take the lead. But she didn't want to lead. Or follow for that matter. She wanted to sit home tomorrow and skip the whole thing. It loomed before her like a huge chasm, or a towering mountain.

How on earth was she ever going to get through the game?

The bleachers were packed on both sides. This was the first game of the season and both sides wanted to win so badly they ached. To vanquish their opponent the first game of the season would put the team in a kind of "we're winners" frame of mind that would stick with them the rest of the season.

The Deep River Killers team was anxious. You could see it in the determined looks on their faces and the frantic way their cheerleaders were trying to whip the fans into a pregame frenzy.

No one wanted the Tarenton Wolves to win more than the Varsity Cheerleaders. If the Wolves won, it would be a shared victory, half of which the cheerleaders could claim since it would be they who were responsible for exciting the fans to wild, enthusiastic support. If the Wolves won, the squad won. Anything less would be devastating.

The cheerleaders were standing in a line, facing the stands. Ardith and Olivia had already decided that they would save their spectacular combination cheer for one of two possible situations during the game: If, horror of horrors, it looked like the Wolves were losing and needed a shot in the arm; or if, and much better, they were winning and needed the fans to cut loose and roar them to a successful finish.

Tara felt tense, but excited and proud. To be standing in front of the crowd, in her red and white uniform, was a dream fulfilled, something that practice, while satisfying in its own right, had never approached in terms of giving her the ultimate thrill. To be in front of the fans, feeling all that excitement and expectation radiating out from them, knowing they were going to be watching every move she made, and knowing as she did, that she'd look sensational, was, well, indescribable.

She looked down the line of cheerleaders, waiting for the moment to arrive when the players would begin streaming onto the field. They would lead the fans in applauding every one of the guys as they were introduced.

She couldn't wait to get started! She saw Jessica bite her lip and wondered if Jessica was excited or nervous.

Jessica spotted Patrick Henley in the stands. He was sitting beside Pres Tilford. Patrick winked at her and blew her a kiss, then made an okay sign with his thumb and forefinger. She smiled widely at him and quickly sent back a V for Victory sign. It was nice having him there as her own, personal supporter. She wondered if Mary Ellen had appreciated Patrick last year. Or if she missed him now.

A movement at the side of her vision snared

her attention and she looked to see what it was. Peter was holding Hope's hand, giving it a reassuring squeeze.

Funny, Peter thought, here I'm so nervous about our first "public" appearance, but I'm playing the cool, it'll-be-okay kid to Hope. The weak supporting the weak. Maybe it would make him strong. Maybe he'd have to play the part so much, he'd actually begin to believe it.

He glanced down the line, saw Sean, and expelled a sigh. Believe it, he thought with a touch of anger. Sean had never been a cheerleader, but right then he looked like he'd never been anything else all his life. The guy practically exuded confidence from his pores like everyone else perspired. It made Peter feel so frustrated.

Suddenly the players began pouring out onto the field.

Well, here goes, Peter thought. Let's see what we can do!

CHAPTER 11

It was the beginning of the fourth quarter. The Deep River Killers were ahead by three points. Both teams had just broken huddles and were lining up for the scrimmage. Their faces were set like granite, each team member knowing that three points was not much of an edge.

Tara stood on the sidelines, feeling so tense and anxious you'd think the team that lost would be punished by being sent to the guillotine instead of merely to the showers.

This wasn't just a silly old game, she thought. This was life or death. Victory over failure. Tara hated failure. She even hated the word *failure*. She couldn't bear being associated with a team that lost. She'd known, of course, when she'd tried out for Varsity, that the Tarenton teams could not be expected to achieve one-hundred-percent success. But she'd hoped they would anyway. At least for their *first* game. In two weeks they would take on their arch rival, Garrison, and she knew if the Wolves lost today they'd be so demoralized they might actually do the unthinkable, *and lose to Garrison*. And that Tara couldn't endure.

"Come on, Wolves! Show 'em your bite!" she screamed at the top of her voice.

This was the signal for the cheerleaders to go into their special cheer, and Olivia was the one who was supposed to have given it. But Olivia seemed to be under some kind of spell and Tara wasn't about to let the Wolves fight for victory without Varsity support. Tara glared at Olivia, while Olivia seemed to mentally shake herself, then nod at the rest of the cheerleaders who'd been watching her closely.

They moved into action. It was time for the cheer they'd been saving. The crowd-pleaser. The crowd-instigator. Time to pull out all the stops.

They lined up, the guys with megaphones, the girls with pompons, one in each hand. The girls began rotating their arms like windmills, making the pompons describe blurry circles in the air.

Six voices raised in unison as they wound themselves up to a fever pitch.

> "Come on, Wolves —
> Show 'em your bite!
> Come on, Wolves —
> Let's fight, fight, fight!"

81

They went into the routine they'd been practicing so hard. Sean placed his megaphone down and turned to Jessica, cupping his locked hands in front of her. She placed her sneakered foot in the stirrup he formed, and he sent her vaulting skyward. She tucked in her knees and did a mid-air backward somersault to land with a bounce on both feet before sliding into a split. Behind her, Sean had performed an accompanying stationary flip followed by a straddle jump.

At the other end of the lineup, Olivia and Peter had mirrored Sean and Jessica, performing the exact same maneuver in unison with them.

Between the two couples, Tara and Hope yelled out the rest of the cheer while juggling their pompons back and forth to each other. The swirling white and red streamers of the pompons flashed brilliantly in the sunlight, looking like flames as they were tossed and retrieved by both girls.

"Come on, Wolves —
Show 'em your stuff.
It's time to kill the Killers,
And really get tough!"

The fans rose to their feet and joined the cheerleaders as they lined up, doing forward cartwheels with precision timing to stand in one clean line in front of the bleachers. Over five hundred voices thundered back:

"Come on, Wolves —
Show 'em your bite!
Come on, come on,
Let's fight, fight, *fight!*"

Hands clapped, feet stomped, making the stands tremble, and the cheerleaders went into the second half of their display, this time with Tara and Hope weaving between the other four, tossing the pompons over their heads in a perfectly orchestrated manner so they never touched either Jessica's or Olivia's flying bodies.

And suddenly Rex Granger, one of the defensive ends, threw himself into the perfect position to steal the ball from the Killers. He charged down the field, flinging bodies away from himself as if he were a tornado.

The fans lost all semblance of control. A few of the guys raced out of the stands to stream down the sideline, as if by being on field level, Rex would be incited to run faster, farther, and more powerfully.

By now he had twenty yards to go and one of the Deep River halfbacks vaulted at his ankles. Rex shook him off as if he were merely an annoying stray dog.

"The guy's a charger!" Sean yelled, punching the air with one fist. *"Go! Go!"*

The other cheerleaders caught up the chant. *"Go! Go!"*

The fans took it up and the sound was almost deafening.

"Go! Go!"

And go Rex did. The distance between himself
and the goal line shrank. Ten yards. Five. *Touchdown!*

Pandemonium broke out. Referees were blowing their whistles all over the place. Fans were
threatening to spill out onto the field. Rex was
strutting around, slapping all his teammates'
hands with his own victoriously upraised one.

Coach Cooley got the Wolves under control
and herded his overexuberant extra team members back to the bench. Those left on the field
spread out into a proud line, preparing for the
kick.

The Deep River Killers faced them in a resent-
ful string. Tempers were only barely under control.

At the signal, Arne Stevenson ran forward and
kicked the ball up, up, and over their opponents'
angry heads. It sailed cleanly between the goal
posts.

The Tarenton fans went wild again, but the
cheerleaders had fanned out into a string with a
lot of pompon waving and high kicks in an effort
to contain anyone in the crowd who hoped to
race out onto the field. The human fence worked.

Now the score was twenty-one to seventeen, in
favor of the Wolves, and there were only three
minutes remaining in the game.

Sean looked at his fellow cheerleaders.

"How about that? We did it! We got this crowd
really going!" He danced over to Tara and lifted
her in a victory stance, his hands on her waist,

making her hands rest on his shoulders while her legs were flung out behind her.

She loved it, taking advantage of the situation to let go of Sean's shoulders and arch her back. Sean twirled around in an impromptu cheer.

Not to be outdone, Peter grabbed Olivia and flung her up. Her year of experience made her react perfectly, but as he set her down, she felt shaky. What was the matter with her? She should be feeling as jubilant as the rest of the squad, but yet she didn't. Instead, she felt flat, like a sour note in the middle of a beautiful sonata. Why?

She turned toward the squad, saying, "Let's get ready to do the 'Victory' cheer." But even saying that caused a curious twisting pain. She realized it was because it wasn't the *old* "Victory" cheer from last year, but a new one — one the fans weren't even familiar with.

They, like she, had to learn a whole slew of brand-new cheers.

But now it would be the Killers' turn to take possession of the ball. They'd have to work awfully hard to earn seven points and they knew it. It wasn't impossible, but it was hardly likely.

The teams lined up at the twenty-five-yard line and Tarenton kicked off to the Killers. In an effort to keep them from scoring, Tarenton's kicker deliberately aimed the ball way back toward the ten-yard line. None of the Killers could reach it in time to catch it, and it hit the turf and bounced.

Then one of the Wolves, astonishingly, pounced on it and downed it right on the Killers' own two-yard line!

This time the cheerleaders were so busy going wild themselves they didn't lead the fans; they just yelled along with them.

"Oh, man!" Sean crowed. "The Killers will never carry that ball ninety-eight yards in the time left." He turned to watch the action as it continued.

In the two and a half minutes remaining in the game, the Wolves used every defensive maneuver they knew to keep the Killers from going anywhere.

The final whistle blew, and the Wolves had won their first game!

The cheerleaders moved into action even though the screaming fans hardly noticed. Why had she been worried about their catching on to new chants? Olivia wondered. The fans weren't even listening to them.

They bounced through the cheer with feet and legs seemingly set free from gravity. Jessica and Sean performed a dazzling display of flips, cartwheels, and straddle jumps, with the rest of the squad moving around them as if they were dancers. Pompons swirled and voices yelled.

"Who are the winners?
Tarenton!
Who aren't beginners?
Tarenton!"

The squad broke out in various shouts and screams, accompanying the rowdy fans who were swarming down from the stands and engulfing the Wolves. They bore Rex off the field on their shoulders.

People spilled past the cheerleaders, who stood, exchanging congratulatory remarks with each other and some of the fans.

"What a play Rex made!"

"Won our first game! All-r-i-g-h-t!"

"Look out Garrison!"

"Garrison's doomed!"

"I'll say. Did you see . . . ?"

Olivia was the only one not caught up completely in the euphoria. She gathered her pompons and prepared to thread her way back to the school to shower and change.

"Hey, Olivia, wait up!" Jessica called.

Curious, Olivia turned and saw the five cheerleaders clustered together along with Patrick and Pres.

"Isn't it traditional to go out and celebrate our victory?" Jessica asked, her green eyes dancing. Patrick's arm was draped over her shoulder. It caught at Olivia's heart. How many times had she seen Patrick's arm draped over Mary Ellen?"

"Yes," Olivia said. "I guess so."

"Well, let's do it." Jessica looked at the others. "Where to, gang? The Pizza Palace? The Burger Hut?"

"Hey, for sure. Let's cel-e-brate!" Sean sang. He clasped his hands together over his head in a triumphant posture.

There were various sounds of agreement, then

seven pairs of eyes focused on Olivia. She stared back at them. Sean, Tara, Jessica, Hope, and Peter.

And Patrick and Pres.

There was something wrong about all this.

Visions of all the after-game gatherings during the previous year swam in Olivia's mind. But it was Angie, Mary Ellen, Nancy, and Walt she saw with Patrick and Pres. Especially Walt.

Olivia choked down a lump in her throat and said tightly, "Um, you go ahead. I've — I've got something I have to do."

"What?!" Pres exploded. "Olivia — "

"Sorry!" Olivia interrupted and spun on her heels. She walked away from the group, tuning out anything more anyone might say to her.

She just couldn't. She just could not endure a "victory" celebration when she felt the way she did. She missed Angie, Nancy, and Walt. Even Mary Ellen. Somehow it just didn't seem right that Patrick and Pres were taking up with the new group of cheerleaders when they didn't even go to the school anymore. Somehow it seemed vaguely traitorous. And if there was one thing Olivia didn't feel up to right now, it was fraternizing with more traitors. She'd had enough exposure to one today already.

CHAPTER

12

And that was what was partly responsible
for Olivia's melancholy.

Right before leaving the house for the game
this afternoon, she had received a letter from
Walt. In it he'd told her that in view of the agreement they'd reached about dating others, he'd
started doing that at college. No one special, he
said, just different girls he'd met. How was she
doing? Any new guys in her life? It had pained
her that he could ask that question with so little
concern. Didn't he miss her at all?

Traitors. The world seemed full of them.

Now all she wanted to do now was go home.
Maybe take a short nap before trying to figure
out that calculus homework. It, like all of her
subjects this year, was becoming difficult to grasp.

She reached for the door to the school, preparing to enter the sanctuary of relative peace of-

fered inside, but was arrested by Mrs. Engborg's voice.

"Olivia! Wait!"

Olivia turned to see Ardith approaching with the firm stride of a military commander about to invade a country. What was up?

"Olivia," Ardith said more gently as she reached her. "After you've changed, please come to my office." Ardith's expression gave no hint of what was on her mind.

"Why?" Olivia's guard came up. In the past Mrs. Engborg had never called any kind of conference in her office unless she'd felt something was amiss.

Ardith's gaze flickered under Olivia's direct one.

"I just want to discuss something with you. Please don't forget." With that, Ardith opened the door and the two of them stepped into the dimly lit school corridor.

Olivia silently walked down the hall to the stairs leading to the girls' locker room. What was up? Why did Ardith want to talk to her? And about what? Were the other members of the squad going to be present?

Olivia was in the shower when she heard the other girls come into the locker room. The Pompon Squad was there, too, so the noise level rose sharply. It grated on her nerves.

Quickly she toweled herself off and headed for her locker. She set a record for speedy dressing, half listening to all the talk flowing around her.

"Pres said he could squeeze one more person

in the Porsche," Tara was saying. "Of course, it will have to be a tiny one to fit between the seats. Hope, do you — "

Hope laughed. "No way. I'm going with Peter and Jessica in Patrick's truck."

It was Jessica's turn to laugh as she teased, "You're turning down a chance to ride in a Porsche just so you can go in a moving van? Goodness! What do you suppose is the attraction?"

She and Hope giggled.

"Well, whoever gets dressed first and gets on the road can save us a booth or two at the Pizza Palace," Tara said.

So they weren't going to be in on the little conference Ardith was calling, Olivia thought. Was that because she was captain and Ardith didn't want the others to hear what she had to say? Did she have some sort of criticism of the squad's performance today? It was a possibility, although they had done all right. Maybe not as well as they could have, but after all, it had only been their first game. They'd probably get better. At least Olivia hoped so.

She closed her locker and left the room, her sport bag clutched tightly in her hand. Now to get this over with.

Ardith's door was ajar and she was sitting at her desk reading something that looked like papers in an opened manila folder.

Olivia shoved the door open wider and stepped into the office.

"Mrs. Engborg? What's up?" she asked as she came to stand uncertainly beside the desk.

Ardith looked up, obviously startled by Olivia's quiet entrance. She quickly closed the folder and placed it in her top desk drawer before waving a hand at the chair pulled up to the other side of her desk.

"Sit down, Olivia," Ardith ordered, although not unkindly.

Olivia sat — perched was more like it — on the extreme edge of the chair. She reminded Ardith of a doe in the woods, poised for flight at the slightest cause for alarm.

"What do you want to talk to me about?" Olivia asked in her direct manner.

"I was hoping you could tell me," Ardith said gently.

"What?" Olivia frowned at her coach.

"Olivia, how good of a memory do you have?" Ardith asked.

Olivia was totally perplexed. What was going on here? She shrugged. "I don't know. A good one, I guess. Why?"

"Then think back and try to remember how you felt about cheerleading at the beginning of school last year." Ardith regarded Olivia with unblinking eyes. Olivia felt as if some sophisticated machine were peeling away the layers of her brain, probing, delving, trying to uncover her secret thoughts. It made her feel defensive.

"Why?"

"Can you honestly tell me you feel the same way this year as you did last year?"

Olivia swallowed, her fingers plucking at the straps of her sport bag. She didn't answer right away and Ardith didn't push. Finally, Olivia slid back in the chair, resting her weary spine against the hard wood. "No. I can't," she said shortly.

"What's wrong then? Can you tell me what's bothering you?"

Startled at Mrs. Engborg's evident concern, Olivia looked at her, then away. She licked her lips nervously, but didn't answer. She couldn't. She really didn't know quite how to put her feelings into words.

"Olivia, I'm going to talk to you like your mother," Ardith began.

Oh, help! Olivia thought. That's the last thing I need.

Ardith saw the expression of distaste cross Olivia's face and knew she'd said the wrong thing. "Okay, pretend I'm a favorite aunt. . . ."

Considering she didn't have one, that would certainly strain her imagination, Olivia thought dryly.

"You seem very unhappy this year. Do you miss last year's squad?"

Olivia shifted in her seat, feeling extremely uncomfortable. What was she supposed to say? "Of course," she answered, sounding defiant.

"That's okay. You're allowed to miss them. After all, you six worked together five days a week practicing cheers, you performed as a unit at all the games, and you certainly shared a social life." Ardith's tone was not one of censor, and

Olivia relaxed. Maybe she did understand after all.

"But," Ardith continued, and Olivia felt her guard come up again, "you know, this year's squad has to have all those things in common, too." Olivia didn't look particularly moved, so Ardith used a different tactic. "Look, the old squad was a great one, but you are the only one left. It's time to look forward to the future, not dwell on the past. It's natural for you to miss your old friends with whom you worked and grew close, but they are all off taking on new things in life and you should be doing the same. Get to know the new squad. They are your contemporaries, your age. With the exception of Hope, who's a junior.

"Do you remember what it was like to be the junior member on the squad while all the rest were seniors?" Ardith added.

Olivia looked at her, confused by this. What did that matter? She'd been a superior gymnast and her age hadn't affected her performance.

"That's right. You were darned good," Ardith continued, revealing an uncanny ability to read Olivia's mind. "And I'm not saying you're not good this year, but you lack the pizzazz you had last year. You have to put the past behind you. Olivia, you are the captain. You must concern yourself with the *new* squad. Since you're the experienced member, they look to you for an example, and even praise. You say something derogatory about them and it hurts." Olivia snorted, and Ardith slammed her palm down on her desk, scaring her. "I mean it! Some of them are especially vulnerable. Like Hope."

"Hope? But she's okay."

"Just okay?"

"Well, I guess she could do a little better, but she's pretty good for her first year," Olivia admitted after a moment of thought.

"Have you told her?" Ardith asked bluntly.

"Told her?"

"Yes, told her. Given her a pat on the shoulder, et cetera, to make her feel less inferior."

"She feels inferior?" Olivia was truly surprised by this.

Ardith struggled to keep a lid on her temper.

"This illustrates just how much of a wall you've managed to put up around yourself. Look around you. Hope needs your support. And the others need help, too, even if they won't admit it. You are their captain; there is a tremendous responsibility in that position. Think of Mary Ellen. Did she ever let her emotions get in the way of her duties as captain?"

Olivia thought about that a few minutes and had to admit that no matter what had been going on in Mary Ellen's private life, she'd been a superb captain. She'd truly loved cheerleading and had never let anything that was bothering her hamper her performance. Cheering her team on to victory had been the only concern for her at all times. Ardith expected the same thing from Olivia, and Olivia knew it. But at the moment she felt so tired and defenseless. She didn't want to be nagged. She just wanted to go home and rest.

"I'll think about what you said," Olivia said, standing and grabbing her sport bag in a white-knuckled grip. "I'll see you Monday at practice." She turned to go. Ardith opened her mouth to say more, but something about the way Olivia stood, almost stooped and beaten-looking, made her decide to leave it for some other time, perhaps when Olivia didn't have a strenuous game behind her.

"All right," Ardith said gently. "But think about the others, too, Olivia."

Olivia just nodded and moved out of the office as quickly as her tired body could go.

She mounted the stairs to the lobby level of the school. The other cheerleaders. They didn't need her. They were doing just fine without her. This is awful, Olivia reflected. Here I am going home to hibernate, while they're all going out to celebrate. Without me. And probably loving it.

But they had asked her to go. They'd all stood there after Jessica brought up a celebration, waiting for Olivia to — what? Take the lead? Show some enthusiasm?

And what had she done? Turned her back on them. Sent them off without her. What a terrific captain she was! If she were to go find them right now, Olivia was positive she wouldn't be welcomed.

96

CHAPTER

Patrick hopped down from the cab of the truck and went around to open Jessica's door.

"You're so old-fashioned and gallant," she told him as he swung the door open for her. Then he held out his arms like a cradle and said, "Jump!"

"Well, not totally old-fashioned. Crazy might be a good word," she said laughing as she jumped. Swinging her legs up and out, she landed in his outstretched arms, cradled against his wide chest. With a grin he swung away from the cab and kicked the door shut with one foot before setting her on her feet.

"Bravo!" Hope applauded. "Great catch. You could be a cheerleader yourself."

"Why didn't you try out last year?" Peter asked in jest, silently thinking, I'd rather have Patrick on the squad than Sean any day.

"Because I graduated," Patrick pointed out good-naturedly.

"How thoughtless of you," Jessica said in mock reproof. "Why didn't you work it out so you flunked? Then you could have been a cheerleader."

"I couldn't be a cheerleader if I flunked," Patrick reminded her with a lopsided grin.

She stood before him, her hands on her hips. He took one of her arms, threaded it through his, and guided her into the Pizza Palace, where the four of them pounced on the last remaining booth.

Sean was coming in his own car, and Tara and Pres in the Porsche. When the last three joined them, there wasn't a seat left in the place. Patrick had pulled up a chair where he'd parked his big frame at the end of the table. Peter, Hope, and Jessica took up one bench seat in the booth, while Pres, Tara, and Sean slid into the other. Tara was flanked on one side by Pres, and on the other by Sean.

"Cozy!" she remarked at the cramped quarters.

"But this real estate's all ours," Patrick said. "Best we could do. Besides, we're closest to the kitchen. Our pizza won't get cold because our waitress won't have to fight her way through the mob to bring it to us."

"Good thinking," Jessica smiled at Patrick.

"When it comes to food, I'm always thinking," he said to her, thinking how relaxed and easy it was with Jessica, compared to the thrust-and-parry relationship he'd always had with Mary Ellen.

Samantha Gray came up to their booth, one of the football players behind her. "Well, guys, I guess you did it. You got the crowd really going." Her gaze swept over the booth, then she frowned. "Where's your captain, Olivia?"

The others exchanged looks, which spoke volumes, and then Hope said with forced brightness, "Oh, she had some errands or something she had to do. She couldn't join us *this* time." She tried to make it look like things would be different next time, but found it difficult to believe herself.

"Oh, that's too bad. Your first game and a victory at that, and she can't be here to celebrate," Samantha said sincerely.

The cheerleaders shared rather grim looks, but said nothing.

Sean studied Samantha's cool, ash-blonde beauty. If he weren't interested in Tara, he supposed she would be worth making a play for. But not now. He had a score to settle.

Samantha and her date faded into the crowd, and everyone sat there, not sure what to say next.

Tara shook her head, making her shiny red hair fall behind her shoulder. She slanted a look at Pres and inquired sweetly, "So, what are we going to do next weekend?"

Beside her, Sean stiffened.

Pres smiled lazily back at her. He recognized her ploy for what it was.

"*Next* Friday night?" he asked, not giving anything away.

Tara pretended to look disappointed, careful to keep her face averted from Sean.

"Oh, no, sorry. I meant Saturday. I can't go out next Friday. Sean's taking me to Chez Marcel."

"Chez Marcel?" Pres asked in surprise. Sean must be raiding his piggy bank to take her there.

"Have you heard of it?" Sean baited, trying to look less antagonistic than he felt.

Pres grinned wider. "Sure. Been there lots of times. It's a favorite haunt of my parents. We're always having some family bash there."

"At the restaurant?" Tara asked, impressed.

"In a room in the back. It's a special place for private parties. Not everyone knows about it. It's okay, but not my style." Pres made the remark as if he were talking about some greasy spoon, implying that the place to which Sean was taking Tara was severely lacking.

Sean bristled and snapped, "Oh? What's the matter, is the place too good for you?"

Tara heard the hostility in his voice and was inwardly pleased. Two boys fighting over their dates with her. It made her feel special.

Pres leaned forward ever so slightly and fixed Sean with a bored, disinterested look. "Not really. I'd say it was the other way around."

Before Sean's rebuttal could cross his lips, Jessica moved into action. She'd been sitting there in fascination, along with the others, but had decided things were heating up just a little too much.

Grabbing one of the large, over-sized menus, she raised it between Sean and Pres so they couldn't see each other. She let out a shrill whistle

100

between her teeth like her older brothers had taught her.

"The ref has just thrown down the flag, boys. Time out."

Everyone sat there, waiting.

Tara didn't look directly at either one of the guys, but she used her peripheral vision to watch their reactions. Jessica was something else, trying to use humor to diffuse the situation, but Tara wasn't sure it would work. She pressed her lips together tightly, to keep from smiling.

Pres looked at the menu, then at Jessica, and was the first to give in. He started chuckling. "Good call, Jessica."

Everyone looked at Sean.

Sean let out a deep breath, then forced a smile on his face. "Okay, ref," he said.

Jessica smiled widely, her green eyes sparkling. She was pretty sure Sean was giving up the fight so he'd appear to be a good sport, not because he wanted to. That keen sense of competition that had made him beat out other guys to be a Varsity Cheerleader was responsible for his desire to beat out Pres for Tara's affections. Everyone knew what was going on. Jessica just didn't want anything to spoil the gay mood that had been brought on by the victory over Deep River.

Just then two large pizzas, one with everything and one with only pepperoni, were placed down on their table by the waitress. She looked harried and overworked. "Drinks are coming up," she said, and raced off.

"Dive! Dive!" Patrick cried as if he were a submarine commander. His big hand swooped in and collected a slice of pizza, but instead of wolfing it down, he handed it to Jessica. "To our little peacemaker," he said in a voice only she could hear.

She smiled, and made a tiny bow for his eyes only.

Everyone began attacking the pizza.

In a quiet voice, Pres said to Tara, "Guess you're free next Saturday." It was a statement of fact. Even if she weren't, Pres expected Tara to break whatever plans she had to go out with him. "Pick you up at seven."

He said nothing more, and between bites Tara watched him, thinking. Playing one boy off against another could prove very interesting. As long as she didn't let it go too far. She wondered what could happen if it did. Would they actually, physically, go at each other? She couldn't imagine Pres ever doing that. But Sean? Of him, she wasn't sure.

She eyed Sean covertly and chewed on her pizza, reflecting on the possibilities. Well, whatever happened, Tara was positive she could handle things if they threatened to get out of hand. If there was one thing Tara understood, it was what motivated boys, and she also had the know-how to deal with them.

CHAPTER

14

Mrs. Bartlet was lecturing the English class on the pitfalls of turning books into movies.

"The main problem screenwriters face is that books tend to deal with what's going on in the main character's head, and it's difficult to portray thoughts on screen without resorting to voice-overs." She adjusted her glasses in a nervous gesture.

"Also, sometimes, in order to make the movie a bigger money maker, they spice it up beyond what the author put in the book. . . ."

She rambled on and Olivia stared at her, thinking, I really don't care about the pitfalls of turning books into movies. I don't get to see movies anymore thanks to Walt, and I'm too busy to read books.

Her gaze shifted to study her classmates. Sean Dubrow sat one row over and two seats ahead of

103

Olivia. She could tell that he was as fascinated by Mrs. Bartlet's dissertation as she was. Instead of using his pen as a writing instrument, he was manipulating it like a tiny baton, agilely twirling it around and around on the tips of his fingers. If I tried that, Olivia thought, the stupid pen would probably fly across the room and then I'd have yet another name to add to the list of teachers who are less than ecstatic with me.

Let's see, Mr. Spencer, Mrs. Engborg. . . . Who next? Probably Mrs. Bartlet, if Olivia didn't try to take some notes like Jessica Bennett was.

Olivia could see Jessica's pen moving back and forth with a speed that would only be possible if she were using shorthand. No one wrote longhand that fast. Jessica seemed to be a girl with an endless string of skills. Which was probably what drew Patrick to her.

Olivia dipped her chin and stared at her almost blank note pad. Patrick. What *did* he think about Jessica? Was he serious about her? To Olivia's mind, it sure looked that way. It worried her. Should she say something or butt out?

Olivia glanced back at Jessica just in time to see her smile secretly at Jim Hanson. Olivia couldn't tell if Jessica was flirting or simply being friendly. Probably Jim didn't know either. Jessica seemed to be very skilled at attracting guys to her side by the droves, while being able to maintain a comfortable distance from them all at the same time. A nice trick, one Olivia wouldn't mind learning. But not if it hurt someone really nice. Like Patrick. What was he doing right now?

Olivia rotated her wrist so she could check the time. Almost noon. Was he on lunch break from his garbage route?

Patrick tied the sweatband he'd fashioned out of a red bandana around his head more securely and paused to take a deep breath. Then he hefted the last garbage can and dumped it in one fluid motion. He placed it down carefully, instead of banging it, and hopped back into the cab of his truck.

Funny, he thought, how things turn out. Here he'd found what appeared to be a girl who embodied all the positive personality traits he'd found lacking in Mary Ellen, but yet she was still apparently missing one extremely important element: the potential to really care about a certain Patrick Henley.

With Mary Ellen it was almost a love/hate thing she'd had for him. When she'd loved him she'd been sensational, warm, affectionate — everything he wanted in a girl. But when she'd hated him, she'd been a witch — self-centered and hypocritical.

And now there was Jessica Bennett, and what did she feel for him? Jessica didn't seem to be particularly serious about starting a relationship with him. She wasn't averse to going out with him, that was easy to see, but the pure emotional response he'd gotten from Mary Ellen was missing. It was obvious Jessica didn't mind being the object of all *his* affection; she just didn't seem to return it. Did that indicate a lack of interest in him on her part? Or that she simply felt it was too early in their relationship — such as it was — to be too serious?

Figuring females out was impossible! Patrick decided to stop for lunch and concentrate on emptying his mind and filling his stomach.

Jessica wandered into the school cafeteria, spotted Tara sitting with Samantha Gray, and decided to skip trying to get all the cheerleaders to sit at the same table at lunch like she'd seen last year's Varsity Squad do. Trying to get this squad to be unified like last year's seemed to be more and more the impossible dream as each day went by. Olivia should be trying to do that, Jessica thought angrily. As captain she was failing. She wasn't assuming command. She was abdicating.

Jessica scanned the lunch room, spotted several people who'd welcome her to their table, then headed for the one at which Hope and Peter sat. Half a squad was better than none. She passed Tara on the way, but Tara seemed to be involved in a heavy discussion with Samantha and didn't even look up.

"So this weekend you go to Chez Marcel?" Samantha asked, her eyes alive with interest. "You must call me, no matter when you get home, and tell me what it was like," she added a little wistfully.

Just beyond Tara's shoulder, Samantha could see Sean Dubrow entering the cafeteria line and begin to choose his food. To go with him, even for a walk, was something most of the girls in school only dreamed of. Samantha said in a light tone to cover the faint envy she felt, "It's simply not fair that you can have two of the best guys in town dating you. Couldn't you do the patriotic thing and share?"

Tara smiled, leaned forward, and said, "It's not *my* choice. Both just seemed to decide they wanted me." She went on to describe in vivid detail the verbal skirmish Sean and Pres had engaged in at the Pizza Palace after the game on Saturday. "So I decided, why not fuel the fire? I mean, maybe I can have a little fun by encouraging each guy to try to outdo the other."

Samantha frowned and said, "Just make sure that if you play with fire, you have an extinguisher handy." She spotted Sean leaving the food line and searching the crowd. He located Tara and began threading through the tables, heading straight for her. "And here comes one of the flames," Samantha said. "Let's just hope you don't get burned."

Tara just laughed. "Don't be silly," she said lightly, and turned to watch Sean approach.

After school, when Tara stepped through the gym doors heading for cheerleading practice, Ardith intercepted her.

"Tara, I want to speak with you privately," Ardith said, taking Tara's arm. "Come with me."

Tara was too inexperienced in dealing with Ardith to know if Mrs. Engborg's blank expression masked her feelings about something good or bad. She simply followed the coach as she was led back out through the door and a few feet down the hall.

Ardith turned and spoke sternly.

"I don't want to see what happened last Saturday again."

"What?" Tara's eyebrows rose in consternation.

"*You* deciding which cheer to use and when. That is the captain's exclusive job — "

"But, Mrs. Engborg, Olivia was asleep at the switch. She wasn't doing anything. She was in a trance or something!"

"Then you might have suggested it to her, not taken it upon yourself."

"But — "

"*No* excuses. In the future, it is your job to *follow* Olivia's lead, not usurp it." Mrs. Engborg glowered at Tara. "Is that understood?"

Tara remained silent a moment. If things were normal, Ardith would be right. But how could Tara be expected to follow a captain who seemed to turn comatose at the game? It was too early in the year for Tara to try to argue with Mrs. Engborg, since she didn't have a clue as to how successful she'd be. Besides, perhaps Mrs. Engborg would see for herself what a dud Olivia was and have everyone vote for a new captain. It would work better for her own chances if Tara looked cooperative.

"Yes, Mrs. Engborg," she said quietly, looking down at her feet.

Ardith had seen it all; she wasn't fooled by Tara's seeming meekness. This one, she knew, would merit watching. And handling with a tight rein.

"All right. Let's get to work."

Ardith led the way back into the gym.

As Tara trailed after her, she was thinking about that all-important game coming up in less than two weeks against Garrison. For that game they'd need a strong squad captain more than anything. Good cheerleading wasn't simply a matter of a few pompon waves in the air accompanied by a couple of rah-rahs. It involved important strategy, and knowledge of crowd psychology. The team could be energized by an enthusiastic crowd of fans, but those fans needed to be whipped up by an effective cheerleading squad.

Olivia had better get her act together before the game with Garrison, Tara fretted. Something *had* to snap her out of this weird mood she'd been in lately by the time of the game. Or it would be too late!

CHAPTER

Sean let himself into the house with his own key. He found a note from his dad taped to the refrigerator, telling him he had a late business appointment that involved dinner. Sean was to fend for himself, eating whatever he could find.

Another night alone with only records and the tube for company. Who cares, Sean asked himself. Since his mother had died he'd gotten used to it.

He opened the refrigerator to see what Windy, their housekeeper, had left before she went home. He grimaced. A quiche sat on the middle shelf. What did that woman think he and his dad were? Wimps? He was starved. After that strenuous cheerleading practice, he needed real food, not *quiche*. Meat and potatoes — that's what Sean wanted. A double burger and fries. Yeah! Perfect.

Sean shut the fridge door and reached into his

pocket for his keys. He pulled them out and tossed them into the air. Spinning on the balls of his feet, he did a half pirouette quickly and caught the keys one-handed behind his back.

Hey neat! What a great move. He ought to figure out how to do that in a cheerleading routine. Maybe catch the megaphone that way instead of the keys. In fact, a sharp move like that could jazz up a dull routine. Half the maneuvers Mrs. E. had him doing were dull. It shouldn't be too difficult to analyze which routine was the dullest and needed this little move he'd just invented to snap it up. He'd think about it and maybe at the next game, he'd use it. Or perhaps he'd save it for that big one with Garrison. Garrison had twelve female cheerleaders. Wouldn't *they* be impressed when he demoed his new trick.

Sean smiled to himself, repeated the key-toss maneuver, and sprinted out the front door. Hamburger Heaven, heat up those grills, he thought. Here comes one hungry guy.

Briefly, Sean considered calling Tara to see if she wanted to come with him, but he rejected that thought as soon as it surfaced in his mind. For one thing, she had a normal family life and no doubt right now she was sitting down at the dinner table with her parents. And, too, he'd seen Tara leave school in Pres's Porsche. It drove him crazy the way that guy always seemed to appear just in time to get Tara first. The only time Sean could be guaranteed to have Tara all to himself was at lunch in school. And he wouldn't put it past Pres to start showing up for that soon, either.

Sean scowled and unlocked his sleek, red Pontiac Fiero — not on the same level as a Porsche, but no slouch of a car either. It was obvious getting Pres off the scene wasn't going to be as easy as Sean had hoped. He guessed he'd just have to try harder.

A few minutes later Sean guided his car into the parking lot of Hamburger Heaven. Not a great place for food, but it was fast and Sean was famished.

He parked, hopped out, and headed toward the building. Then he lurched to a stop and stared, hardly believing his eyes.

There inside, snuggled in a booth, talking, laughing, and eating, were Pres and Tara! What was Tara doing there instead of at home?

Anger boiled inside Sean and made him turn and wrench open his car door. He dropped into the seat and sat there, fuming, trying to get his emotions in check.

What should he do? Go crash their little party? Or go home to quiche? Neither idea appealed to him. In fact, just seeing the two of them in there, all comfy and cozy, made his appetite vanish.

He slammed his fist into the steering wheel, then started up the car, and headed for home via the long route — out along Fable Point, then around Narrow Brook Lake — driving fast and maybe even a little recklessly to try to put the vision of Tara and Pres, their heads close together, out of his mind. There just *had* to be some way he could show Tara that he was better than Pres. But how?

Sean would be taking her to Garrison to the most expensive restaurant he could think of. Then to a club for dancing. He'd just have to put on the charm that night and make Pres look like a very dull boy.

Tara stood in front of her long mirror, assessing her looks. Now that she had found out where Sean was taking her — to Chez Marcel! — she knew exactly what to put on. Thank goodness it was still warm enough for her to wear her mauve dress with the narrow straps and plunging back. Of course, she was wearing over it a stylish flowered oversized jacket with dropped padded shoulders. But later, when they got to the club, that jacket would go and she knew her dress would show off one of her best features — great skin, even on her back and shoulders.

Her sandals, which weren't more than a couple of strips of mauve leather, had three-inch-high heels. Those sandals were so sexy, even her feet looked terrific in them!

Swirling, Tara observed the effect in the mirror. She liked the way the full skirt with its dropped waist flared out and showed a couple of extra inches of leg. Attention grabbing! She was ready for whatever the evening held.

Her parents were downstairs waiting to see how she looked. Snatching up a mauve clutch purse, she descended the stairs, feeling special, like royalty. Nothing could pop the bubble of pleasure she felt building inside her chest.

Entering the living room where her parents sat,

Tara swirled dramatically and then flung out her arms like a model as she came to a stop right in front of them.

"What do you think?" she asked, expecting to hear the usual compliments.

"Lovely, dear," her mother said.

Her father frowned slightly, but only said, "You certainly look grown-up in that outfit." He smiled. "I don't know that I'm ready to lose my special little girl."

"Oh, Dad," Tara laughed. "I'm going out to eat, not to elope." She bent to plant a kiss on his cheek, then straightened abruptly as a horn sounded outside.

The frown settled on his face again. "Is that your date?"

"Of course, Dad," Tara said, turning to kiss her mother good-bye.

"I don't approve of boys who simply honk," he said sternly.

Tara rolled her eyes as she turned away.

"I understand from your mother," he continued, "that the young man who came for you last week did the same thing. If I'd been here I wouldn't have allowed you to go out at a rude honk." He stood and strode toward the door.

"Oh, Daddy, that's old-fashioned. It's all right. I don't mind." Tara was getting edgy. She was thinking to herself, I'll just bet you'd have made Pres come to the door last week! *If* you had been here. But like so *many* nights, you were still at work.

"Manners are not old-fashioned," her father

grumbled. He went to the front door and glared out at the red Fiero.

Tara quickly slid by him and said, "Don't worry. I'll tell Sean next time to come to the door."

"I should hope so," her father muttered.

How like him to care about the boy's manners, Tara thought a little bitterly. Instead of his prime interest being her having a good time, he was grousing about Sean's *manners*, concentrating on appearances rather than feelings. Tara wanted her father's attention centered solely on *her*, not diffused by irritation over Sean's manners or lack of them. And what was the big deal about honking anyway?

Tara forced a smile on her face as she approached the passenger side door. Sean didn't get out of the car but simply leaned over and opened the door from the inside.

Please let Dad not see this! Tara thought. He'll hyperventilate.

"Hello, gorgeous," Sean greeted her as she slid into the car. "Ready to boogie?"

"All night long!" Tara wanted to forget the scene with her father. It left a bad taste in her mouth and had popped the bubble of happiness. Sometimes she got so frustrated with her dad. He claimed to dote on her, but he was around so little, what with his sixty-hour work week, his tennis at the club, and the seemingly endless string of social engagements — even in the middle of the week — that there was precious little time for actual doting.

Tara's parents had had some kind of dinner to attend this past Wednesday night, too, so when Pres had offered to take her home she'd let him know she was going home to an empty house. No need to mention that Marie, their French house-keeper, would be there, no doubt preparing one of Tara's favorite dishes as consolation.

Tara had put on the abandoned waif routine to perfection and when Pres had suggested the two of them grab a bit at Hamburger Heaven, naturally she'd leaped at it.

Still smiling faintly at the memory, Tara turned to her present escort.

Sean was looking over her outfit, which she'd chosen with extreme care. He whistled, then said approvingly, "Check it out! I can see we'll make a dynamite couple out on the dance floor tonight!"

Tara laughed. "But of course. Who could compare with the best-looking couple at Tarenton High?" She said exactly what she knew he'd like to hear, and it achieved the desired effect. Sean grinned, obviously in agreement with that statement.

He looked great, too. If Sean had one talent it was knowing how to dress. His off-white unconstructed jacket was worn with a pair of navy blue pleated slacks and a blue and white pin-striped shirt with a white collar. No tie, which was probably his way of thumbing his nose at convention. Otherwise he looked like any average tycoon's son about to escort a girl out on a fabulous night on the town, Tara thought, stifling a giggle.

"How about one for the road?" Sean suggested, looking at her out of the corners of his dark eyes.

"Huh?" Tara was momentarily confused. Was Sean suggesting they drink? He knew they were supposed to lay off the booze if they wanted to remain on Varsity.

"A kiss, gorgeous. A kiss to start the evening off right," Sean explained lazily. Before Tara could react, he'd covered her mouth with his own in a dramatic, impressive kiss. Tara was amazed and yet not amazed at his prowess. No doubt he got a lot of practice!

He pulled back to study her reaction. He'd put everything he had into that kiss. If that creep Tilford had kissed Tara, Sean wanted his kiss to obliterate any memory of it from Tara's mind.

It produced the exact opposite result. Mentally Tara was comparing them even as she smiled at Sean and said, "Well! The evening ahead is looking more interesting by the minute." Again her calculated response brought the desired reaction.

Sean, grinning widely, said, "Isn't it?" and shifted into reverse, backing out onto the street.

As he drove, Tara contemplated the possibilities. She wasn't exactly sure why Sean's apparent interest in her had suddenly accelerated lately, or why both Pres and Sean seemed to want to win her away from each other. But she was extremely happy to be the prize in this contest — as long as she could continue to pull the strings. The minute it looked like she was losing control of the situation, though, she intended to do something about it. Something that might not make either guy particularly happy. But rather than lose control, and chance having either guy get to see her inner self, which certainly wasn't much compared to the girl she let them see, she was willing to lose both guys.

CHAPTER

 16

Patrick Henley was pumping gas into his moving van at the Mobil station on Main Street when he saw Sean Dubrow's red Fiero flash by. The slanting rays of the setting sun lit up Tara Armstrong's red hair, making it look almost as bright as fire.

So, he thought, the two of them are going out tonight. He wasn't jealous that Sean was out with Tara; he was jealous that either of them was going out at all. Patrick had asked Jessica to go out with him tonight — just for a burger, nothing fancy. But she'd refused. He'd tried, tactfully, to find out if her negative response was because she already had a date, but she'd proved to be remarkably resistant to letting out information. He'd felt like an inept safecracker unable to work the combination lock. He still didn't know why she'd refused, or what she was doing tonight.

It irked him. He told himself it was because her behavior was so Mary Ellen-like, but deep inside he was beginning to suspect that there might be a more personal reason.

He paid for the gas, hopped back into the truck, and headed for home.

One thing he did know: Spending the evening alone wasn't appealing, but he didn't appear to have any other choice. At least tomorrow the Wolves played the Kensington Kings. That should be interesting. He could sit up in the stands and watch Jessica, and perhaps learn from someone — Pres, maybe — just what exactly the deal was with Jessica Bennett.

Jessica sat on the couch in the family room staring glassy-eyed at the television. A commercial about yet another brand-new, "revolutionary" deodorant was on, and she'd muted the sound using the remote control.

Her mother and Daniel were out for the evening. A few weeks ago her brother, Gary, had returned to his army base in California after a quick trip home. Her other brother, John, was away at the college he attended.

Everyone's out having fun and I'm home brooding, she thought.

But it didn't have to be that way. She could have gone out. Instead of leftovers for dinner, eaten in front of the tube, she could have had hamburgers with Patrick.

But she'd shied away from going out with him. He was beginning to make her nervous. He

120

wanted too much of her time, too much of her attention. She felt suffocated. It seemed so obvious to her that what he wanted from her was more than she was prepared to give — more than she wanted in a relationship with *any* guy. In fact, she didn't want any kind of a relationship with any guy whatsoever.

Dating was fine as long as it was kept on a light, friends-only basis. The minute it looked like romance was trying to rear its head, Jessica bolted like a scared rabbit. Romance was just great — for anybody else! Jessica had no intention of hooking up permanently with any guy. Permanent relationships just *weren't* — eventually the guy took off.

Or died.

A familiar pang shot through her as Jessica thought back seven years to the day her father had suffered a heart attack and died. Oh, Daddy! Why did you have to leave us?

With a superhuman will Jessica wrenched her mind away from a subject that invariably brought out the Kleenex box. She turned on the sound to the TV and listened to the game show host hold out ridiculously fantastic prizes as bait for the game contestants to go for. Silly. She hated games. Well, TV games. Football and basketball games were great. And tomorrow was the game against Kensington. After the Wolves' spectacular victory last week, Jessica had no doubts that they'd cream their opponents tomorrow. And she, along with the rest of Varsity Squad, would be right there to incite the fans to enthusiastic and well-deserved support. Now *there* was a positive thought to brighten a generally dreary evening!

Jessica flipped off the TV and headed for her room. Tomorrow — another victory for the Wolves coming up!

It was an away game at Kensington, but despite the fact that it was out of town, the bleachers on the Wolves' side of the field were packed with fans. Students and parents had made the trip, inspired by the knowledge that after last week's victory, another win was easily ahead.

The cheerleaders stood on the sidelines, discussing strategy. Olivia was attempting to shoulder her responsibility as captain and direct the squad, but her lack of total commitment was clearly evident to the others.

Tara was fuming inwardly. How much more proof did Mrs. Engborg need to see that simply because Olivia was the only veteran from last year's squad, that didn't mean she was automatically the most qualified to be captain?

Jessica was oblivious to Tara's turmoil; she was oblivious to everything in fact, except that she'd just caught sight of Pres and Patrick working their way up the center aisle of the stands, looking for seats.

She bent down to pick up her pompons in preparation for the moment when the cheerleaders would lead the fans in greeting the players as they made their first entrance onto the field.

When she straightened, she couldn't prevent herself from glancing at the stands to see where

Pres and Patrick had ended up. Her gaze collided with Patrick's and tiny shock waves coursed through her. To Jessica, Patrick's face looked tortured, even confused. She must have hurt him last night, she thought with a pang of remorse.

Then instantly, as if Patrick had just realized Jessica had seen him, his expression was transformed. He gave her one of his characteristic crazy grins that was half serious, half silly.

That was *not* the look of a man in misery, Jessica told herself. The first expression had probably been indigestion or something.

She waved at him and turned away. So much for thinking her refusal to go out with him last night had been damaging to Patrick. What did she think she was? A *femme fatale* with the power to make guys' lives seem worthless if they couldn't date her?

"Let's go, squad," she heard Olivia call, and noticed the Wolves' football players were beginning to stream out onto the field.

It was half way into the third quarter of the game and the Tarenton fans were sunk into a collective depression. The cheerleaders sat on the sidelines looking as if each one had lost their best friend. The Wolves were losing, and not just by a slim margin — they were being routed. The Kensington Kings had twenty-one points; the Wolves *zero*.

About a third of the Tarenton fans had slunk away, leaving a stalwart group that was determined to stay with the team to the bitter end.

Tara's temper had just blown wide open. "If Olivia would just get off it and choose some cheers to get the fans yelling enthusiastically, the Wolves would realize the crowd does care, that they're behind them, and *then* maybe they'd rally and win!" she complained to no one in particular.

At the moment Olivia was a few feet away talking to Ardith. They both looked glum.

"Tara," Peter said dejectedly. "It's not Olivia's fault. We could all stand on our heads and wave our pompons with our toes, and it wouldn't do any good. This team is thoroughly demoralized. And you can tell that the Kings are just a better team this year — "

"Traitor!" Tara hissed, and turned away. She looked at Sean for support. "What do you think? Do *you* have any school spirit left?"

"I've got plenty of school spirit. But unfortunately Pete's right. The Wolves are just outclassed this year."

"Gee, thanks for the support," Peter said half jokingly and half resentfully. He hated the idea that his opinion apparently didn't have any worth until the great Sean Dubrow backed it up. But at the same time, he was secretly pleased that he and Sean were seeing eye to eye on *something*, even if it was their team's hopeless situation.

Olivia and Ardith came over to the squad. Olivia stood slightly behind and to the side of Ardith and listened while the coach gave the squad a pep talk.

"Now, I know things look horrible. But remember, we have one and a half quarters left and

124

anything can happen to turn the tables. I want you to get up in front of this crowd and root for the team for all you're worth. Show the fans you haven't given up, that you have faith. Show them you're a group with class. And who knows? It might just inspire the team to win after all."

But it didn't. The Wolves remained down in the dumps and when the final whistle blew, the Kings had thirty-four points and the Wolves a paltry three.

As the mass exodus from the stands dwindled to a trickle, the cheerleaders headed dejectedly for their locker rooms to collect their gear before the bus ride back to Tarenton.

No one felt like talking.

And no one suggested any kind of an after-game gathering.

Tara didn't even feel like going out with Pres as planned, which vaguely surprised her. She sopped up male attention like a thirsty sponge, yet tonight she didn't want to be with anyone. When she joined Pres later, in the Kensington High parking lot, he didn't look all that eager to go out, either. They both agreed to cancel the night.

Sean, who exited the school just in time to hear their discussion, smiled to himself. Now would be a great time to move into the vacancy left by Pres. Tara and he would be on the team bus, while Pres would drive back to Tarenton in his car along with his passenger, Patrick Henley. What a perfect opportunity to sit next to Tara and console her.

Losing games held some importance for Sean; he wasn't immune to the aura of despondency on the bus. He just knew there were always losers in any situation in life, whether games or otherwise. It was a natural outcome of the struggle. There were losers; there were winners. And Sean intended to maneuver himself onto the inside track and come out a winner tonight.

CHAPTER

17

Once he was on the bus, Sean plopped down into the seat next to Tara before anybody else did. Hope and Peter took the seat in front of them, Olivia and Jessica behind them. The demolished Wolves flopped and sprawled exhaustedly in various positions, while their coach proceeded to give them one of his You-did-your-best talks.

"Not another It's-not-whether-you-win-or-lose-but-how-you-play-the-game speech," Rex Granger muttered so low only those within a three-foot radius could hear.

While Coach Cooley droned on, Sean said to Tara, "It's too bad Pres couldn't take you home in his car. If it were me, I'd want to be with only you." He stretched his arm along the back of the seat and gave her shoulder a gentle squeeze.

Tara looked at him, not exactly sure how to react. "Oh?" was all she said.

"Yeah. Seems to me after today's game it's a good time to go have a Coke or something in a nice quiet place. To kind of power down, but at the same time gear ourselves up for Garrison."

Tara looked interested and Sean pressed on.

"Yeah, sure, today's defeat will go down in the records of Tarenton High as one of our worst, if not *the* worst. So it's all the more important for us, the cheerleaders, to think of a way to pump the team and the school back up again, to get them ready to slaughter Garrison next week. If the others aren't interested, well that's their choice. But you and I" — he accented this with another shoulder squeeze — "*really* care about this team. We could go someplace out of the way and put our heads together and think up a plan to get the school in an up mood and ready to clobber our opponents." He pulled her closer and asked into her ear, "So what do you think?"

Tara smiled at Sean. "I think you're absolutely right. We cheerleaders are responsible for school morale. We are the ones who have to pump them up again. I've got an idea already."

She started to tap on Peter Rayman's shoulder, when Sean grabbed her hand and held it. He whispered, in a voice designed to suggest intimacy, "Look, why don't you and I just talk it over between *us* at first. Then when we have a concrete plan, we'll tell the others." He looked deeply into Tara's dark, beautiful eyes.

She appeared to consider this. "Okay," she said finally.

Sean's idea was great. If they, with Tara being

128

the big brain behind it as she intended, could come up with a really great plan, then perhaps the others would see that she, not Olivia, had really terrific leadership qualities.

While Sean and Tara talked in low, secretive voices, Hope and Peter sat holding hands.

"I feel like a deflated balloon," Peter said.

"Me, too. It's not so bad to lose once in a while, I guess, but to lose by thirty-one points! It's awful!"

"It's disgusting."

"This is a real downer," Hope sighed, and laid her cheek against Peter's shoulder. "But I guess we'll have to get used to it." She raised her head and smiled wanly at him. "It's funny. It feels so different to experience the Wolves' defeat as a cheerleader instead of simply as a fan. You know, last year I could go home or out with friends and it wouldn't color the mood for the whole night. But this year . . . I feel it's as much a personal defeat as a team one."

"I know exactly what you mean," Peter agreed, surprised that she could put into words perfectly the feelings he had. In so many ways their minds meshed. It made him feel strange and comfortable at the same time to have a female he appeared to share so much with be close to him. It wasn't like with his mother, who since the divorce, made him feel smothered. Hope always seemed to be holding him at a distance, but it was a comfortable distance. It was as if she wouldn't be against their entering a very close relationship, one that could be the closest Peter had ever experienced. And it

129

surprised him that even here, amidst a bus full of dejected players, being with Hope could make him feel so happy.

"What do you say we drown our sorrows over a hamburger after we get back to Tarenton?" he proposed, and Hope eagerly agreed.

"No reason why we have to be alone to feel miserable," she said.

"Right. Misery — "

" — loves company!" they finished in unison, and then laughed very softly as Peter pulled Hope close into his arms.

Jessica sat limply, her head resting against the back of the seat. She was too tired to talk, but Olivia hadn't made any efforts to be the great communicator either, which was fine with Jessica. She'd been somewhat preoccupied today at the game, finding herself unable to keep from glancing up at the stands now and then at Patrick. His carefree expression had hardly ever changed except toward the last half of the game when it had become obvious that the Wolves were being trounced.

So she'd managed to convince herself that things between them could continue the way she wanted, with no demands, no attempts to clip her wings. She'd be free to do whatever she wanted with whomever she wanted. But the oddest thing was, she didn't seem to be feeling indescribable joy over this realization. Still, she was not going to allow herself to become tied down to one guy. It would just set her up for too much pain.

* * *

Tara and Sean took a booth way at the back of the Pancake House. The restaurant was definitely not on the top ten list of favorite hangouts for high school kids, hence their decision to go there. They wanted to hatch their plan undisturbed.

"So, this is my idea," Tara began as soon as they were seated. "We go to Mrs. Oetjen and get her permission to have a special emergency pep rally, either during the last half of lunch break on Friday or right after school."

"But we've got practice after school," Sean pointed out.

"A pep rally would be a form of practice. Ardith shouldn't have any objections to that," Tara insisted confidently.

"Okay, sounds great. If we can get the school pumped up on Friday, the Wolves should be in a winning frame of mind on Saturday. So when do we tell the others?" Sean asked, referring to the absent squad members.

"Well, technically Olivia's the one who should approach the principal for permission. But do you seriously think she'd be convincing?" Tara aimed a look at Sean that expressed her doubts that Olivia could get inspired to do anything. "I mean, was she dead on her feet today, or what?"

"Yeah. There's something wrong with her lately. Last year her cheerleading sent off so many sparks she could have started a fire. This year she's like a dead ember." He frowned as he contemplated Olivia's personality change, then

131

shrugged. "So we'll go to Oetjen ourselves and get the old girl to give us time for a pep rally."

"Right. Then we'll tell the others. We'll get the fans going again!" Tara said and smiled as Sean reached across the table and took her hand in a We're-in-this-together gesture.

Tara was sure that when the news got out, she would be responsible for reactivating the school's broken spirits, and she would win respect, admiration, and maybe, Olivia's job.

Pres cruised through Tarenton leisurely after letting Patrick off at his house. He didn't feel like going home, nor did he feel like stopping off anywhere in town. He knew he'd probably find at least a handful of kids, moping about the game, in all the regular places.

He drove down Main Street and started to pass the Pancake House. A car in the parking lot grabbed his attention. If he didn't know better, he'd say that was Sean Dubrow's red Fiero. But this was definitely not the kind of joint Sean would bother with.

Pres was directly in front of the restaurant when the door opened and out walked Sean — with Tara Armstrong right behind him! Pres wrenched the wheel and turned into the parking lot of the Pancake House. He drove around behind the building and out to the other side. Sean's car was parked on the outside edge of the lot, and Pres managed to cut off Sean and Tara as they were about to cross the lot toward the car. He sat there, a casual look on his face, and watched them.

The whole maneuver had been instinctive; even at that moment Pres wasn't sure why he'd done it. He supposed he wanted Tara to know that she couldn't get away with her little I'm-not-in-the-mood-for-celebrating act back at Kensington.

She approached his open window with Sean practically plastered to her side. Sean wrapped his arm around Tara's waist in a possessive gesture that annoyed Pres. On the outside, he looked amused for Sean's benefit.

"Pres!" Tara said, staring down at him. Her tone gave away nothing. It actually expressed her delight at seeing him. Pres couldn't decide whether she was a very good actress, or really sincere.

"It's a little early for breakfast, don't you think, kids?" he drawled, giving Sean a bored look.

"Don't you mean *late*?" Sean shot back.

"Nope. Early. For *tomorrow's* breakfast." It was a stupid and childish argument, and Pres knew it, but he didn't seem able to refrain from baiting Dubrow.

Obviously Tara also thought the whole thing was silly for she changed the subject, saying, "Sean and I were talking on the bus on the way from Kensington and we decided we had to do something to get everyone at school pumped up again for next weekend's game against Garrison. That's why we were in the Pancake House. We were having an idea session."

133

Tara understood the meaning behind Sean's possessive hold on her waist, but she stepped forward, out of it, and bent down, placing her hands on the top of Pres's door. It was a deliberate move on her part to send the message to Pres that Sean's ownership of her was all in Sean's mind. She knew she could give Sean conflicting signals after Pres was off the scene.

Tara blocked Sean's view of Pres, but he didn't need to see him to know he was irritated that Tara had pulled away from him in front of Pres. Pres smiled that way Tara hated. He knew Tara wasn't interested in Sean, that she could be his in the snap of his fingers. Just knowing that made Pres relax. He hadn't liked feeling jealous of Sean. It was a relief to know he had no cause. That put him back in the driver's seat in his relationship with Tara.

"Oh, yeah? Without the rest of the squad?" he asked lazily.

She frowned a little, but it was Sean who answered. "They weren't interested." It was a small fabrication. They weren't interested because they hadn't been offered the chance to be.

"Oh," Pres said, wondering if that was true. Was this year's squad that disunified? And what about Olivia? "What did you think up?"

"To have a special pep rally next Friday. What do you think?" Tara asked.

"Should work." Pres revved the Porsche's engine. "Well, I have to go. Home and hearth await. See you around." He nodded at Tara in a thoroughly impersonal manner, knowing exactly

134

how it would affect her, and put the car in first.

Sean pulled Tara back against his chest as the Porsche roared away. "Stupid jerk," he muttered. "Could have knocked you down."

Pres glanced in his rearview mirror and smiled. Tara was staring after him, looking troubled. Good. Let her wonder if she'd spoiled things between them. As long as *he* knew the score, she didn't need to.

CHAPTER

18

Mrs. Oetjen allowed the school to have the special pep rally after school, not during lunch, which wasn't completely satisfying to Tara. Some kids would be going on to after-school jobs, or dentist appointments, et cetera, and she wanted as many to show up for the rally as possible. But no amount of persuasion would make the principal change her mind.

"It's too short notice," she told Tara on Monday when Tara and Sean visited her before school. "Teachers have things scheduled during lunch, too, you know. And to have it after school won't affect the day's routine."

They left Mrs. Oetjen's office dissatisfied, but still glad they could announce the permission granted. Rather than have Ardith hear directly about the plan from Tara and thereby lay Tara wide open for another of the coach's lectures on trying to take over Olivia's job, Tara cornered Olivia at lunch and convinced her to "suggest" a pep rally to Ardith. Tara made it look like the two of them were discussing a plan that was only in the formative stages, not an accomplished scheme.

At first Olivia wasn't exactly the picture of wild enthusiasm. "Do you really think a pep rally is going to make the team play better?" she asked at lunch time. Her tone indicated she doubted it.

Tara clenched her fists under the table, but managed to keep her voice level. "Of course. Besides, it can't hurt. And it might even be just the thing to give the team back its confidence." When Olivia still looked dubious, Tara got more emotional. "Olivia! Garrison's always been our main rival. We can't let them beat us the first time we play them."

"*We* aren't playing them, the Wolves are," Olivia said irritably. One part of her was aware that she was being irrational, but she felt so tired lately, the thought of a rally at which she'd have to expend energy made her anxious.

"You know what I mean! We can't fail to do our duty to try to perk up the school's spirit. If we don't try, then we don't deserve to be cheerleaders." Tara stared at Olivia, ready to scream if she didn't agree soon. In one remote part of her brain, Tara was even surprising herself at the vehemence with which she felt the need to champion the Wolves. She realized more was at stake here than simply putting herself forth in a manner that would bring her admiration. She really *wanted* Tarenton to win! I'm not all for self-glory, she told herself, and actually felt rather proud.

"Okay," Olivia said tiredly. "I'll talk to Mrs. Engborg right before practice tonight, and if she says okay, I'll make the announcement."

"Great," Tara breathed in relief. "Look, I'll just run out and ask Mrs. Oetjen if it's okay to hold a rally. Then you only have to approach one person."

"Okay," Olivia agreed, looking at Tara strangely. "Thanks." It surprised her to some degree that Tara wanted to be so helpful and supportive. Maybe she didn't know Tara Armstrong at all.

Tara rose to her feet, feeling victorious, and went to find Sean to tell him stage two of their plan was accomplished.

Olivia sat staring after Tara. One thing no one could ever say, she thought, was that Tara Armstrong didn't take her duties as a Varsity Cheerleader seriously. In fact, the opposite seemed to be true: She acted like failure to carry them out was like rooting for the other team.

Well, she was sure Mrs. Engborg would okay the rally. Why not? Right now anything that could show the Wolves their school believed in them was worthwhile.

Sighing, Olivia stopped playing with the unappetizing food on her plate and stood up. She walked over to the garbage cans and dumped it before putting her tray on the return rack. Why hadn't she, as *captain*, thought of the pep rally? Maybe it was time for her to step down. If she

138

did, the squad would probably choose Tara. Tara didn't have any more experience than the rest of the newcomers, but she certainly had ambition. Was ambition all a captain needed? Was experience *really* all that important?

Olivia headed for her locker to get the books she needed for her afternoon classes.

If Mary Ellen had been here this year *she* would have thought of the rally. She wouldn't have needed one of the other squad members to think it up for her. Olivia felt undeserving of the honor of captain. She was a failure. Not just at being captain of Varsity, but in her school work, too. Next period was social studies and she knew the unit quiz they were going to have in class today was going to give her trouble. Somehow over the weekend it had completely slipped her mind and she'd never studied for it. Maybe she should just lie down and give up.

She turned and caught sight of Jessica Bennett walking down the hall with some guy Olivia couldn't identify from the back. Jessica was laughing, her green eyes turned up to the guy's face. She seemed to be acting very friendly toward him. And that reminded Olivia of another thing that had been bothering her lately. Jessica and Patrick. What should she do, what *could* she do, about them? How could she warn Patrick not to get involved with Jessica because he might get hurt? Or was it too late?

The pep rally was scheduled to take place out on the football field right after school on Friday, and the majority of the student body was able to attend. The cheerleaders were facing the packed stands, getting ready to try to improve the school's spirit. The school's football players were in the stands, too, and as Olivia stepped forward to use the portable microphone, she aimed her first comments at them.

"We know you'll do your best tomorrow, guys, but we hope this rally will inspire you, and make you realize that win or lose, the school's behind you."

"We don't want to hear the word lose, Olivia!" someone in the stands yelled.

Tara snorted, and exchanged looks with Sean.

"Come on, Olivia," Jessica said. "Ignore the hecklers. Let's show them our stuff."

Olivia sighed, and turned toward the squad. "Okay. Let's do the 'Beat It' cheer."

It was a loose adaptation of the words from a Michael Jackson song. With its high energy, kicking, and jabbing moves, it was designed to really fire up the crowd.

The cheerleaders lined up and started in.

Up in the stands, Angie Poletti sat squeezed between Pres and Patrick. She'd come home from college at State for the weekend just an hour ago, and had spotted Patrick's garbage truck almost as soon as she'd entered Tarenton's town limits. She'd been so happy to see him, she'd slammed on the brakes, parked the car in back of the truck, and leaped out to rush up to Patrick to give him a huge hug. She'd learned the news about the pep rally from Patrick and had decided to come see how the new squad was working out. And to surprise Olivia.

As the squad began to perform, Angie decided it was *she* who was surprised. And not pleasantly so. Oh, the five new members really seemed to be putting their all into their performance, but, still, something was wrong. And Angie was afraid she could identify the source of the trouble.

She nudged Patrick on the shoulder. "Patrick, do you notice something different about Olivia?"

Patrick studied Olivia a few seconds, then shrugged. "Like what?"

"Look at her cheerleading. Doesn't it seem to be lacking something?"

Patrick frowned and his mouth turned down in a dubious grimace. "Looks okay to me."

"That's because you don't know her like I do. I practiced and performed with her countless times last year. I know how she looks and acts when she's cheering. I know her smile. And that's not Olivia's smile. That's not Olivia at all. It's a fake."

Patrick echoed, "A fake!" and looked back down at the tiny cheerleader he thought he knew so well. He decided Angie was especially sensitive, because as far as he could tell, Olivia was the same as always.

Angie suddenly stood up, a determined expression on her face.

"Where are you going?" Patrick asked as he tucked in his long legs to allow Angie through.

"To talk to someone who knows Olivia almost as well as I do, to see if I'm imagining things or if Olivia really is different."

Angie pushed her way down the row to the aisle and then descended to the edge of the field. She spotted Ardith in the seat she always had, off to the far right of the stands where she could observe the cheerleading performance.

If something was wrong with Olivia and it wasn't all in her imagination, Angie knew Mrs. Engborg would be the one to talk to. If *anyone* could explain things, Angie was positive it was Ardith.

CHAPTER

19

The rally was finally over. Olivia thought it had been an ordeal. The rest of the squad seemed to think it had been a smashing success. Tara, Jessica, and Hope bubbled with enthusiasm as they showered and changed in the locker room.

Olivia stood in front of her locker, trying to force herself to look as happy as the others felt.

"Tara, it was a great idea," Jessica was saying. "The pep rally really seems to have restored the football team's morale. I can't wait to cheer at the game tomorrow!"

Hope did a spontaneous C jump and agreed. "Yes! I can feel victory coming our way!"

"Thanks," Tara said, feeling good about herself. She'd given out little hints to the squad members during the rally that the idea for it had been hers, and it had paid off. The other girls on the squad thought she was brilliant.

"Don't you think it was a success, Olivia?" Hope called over the lockers.

Olivia hesitated before answering. "It seems to have gotten everyone pumped up," she said carefully. "Of course, the actual game is the important thing. *We* had a couple of pep rallies last year, too, but the team still lost afterward."

Her answer came just as Angie Poletti stepped into the locker room. She'd been just in time to hear it, see the faces of Hope, Jessica, and Tara react to Olivia's comment, and know she had to speak up. She couldn't see Olivia, but she knew Olivia would be able to hear her.

"Of course, we *also* had more pep rallies where the team got so energized they *did* win, and I can tell from the reactions in the stands that you've got a good chance of winning tomorrow. So don't lose your enthusiasm!" She smiled widely at the three new members who stared at her in surprise, then broke out in cheers and applause.

"Right on!" Tara crowed.

"You said it!" Jessica called.

"Angie!" Olivia screamed and burst into sight from behind a bank of lockers. She catapulted across the floor and grabbed Angie in a fierce embrace. The three other cheerleaders gaped. They hadn't seen Olivia this emotional in a long time.

"Olivia!" Angie laughed, delighted and surprised at the ardency of Olivia's response to her arrival.

Olivia was so happy to see Angie she felt like crying. In fact, her eyes actually misted over as

144

she stepped back, feeling embarrassed that she'd reacted so emotionally.

"So tell me how cheerleading is this year," Angie invited, as Olivia took her hand and pulled her back toward her locker.

They talked to each other as Hope, Jessica, and Tara got dressed and then left, one by one, each saying her good-byes to both Angie and Olivia.

Then when the only two left in the locker room were Angie and Olivia, Angie's smile slipped off her face. "Okay, Olivia, now that it's just you and me, why don't you tell me what's wrong? What's bothering you?"

Olivia played dumb. "What do you mean? Nothing's wrong." She turned away and made a display of packing her gym bag so Angie couldn't see her face.

"Come on, Olivia. This is me, Angie, remember? I've been talking to Mrs. Engborg and she's been telling me a few things I don't like hearing."

Olivia looked defensive. "Like what?" she asked with a guarded expression.

Angie sat down on a bench and said, "Sit down, Olivia. Let's talk this out — "

"There's nothing to talk out — "

"Yes, there is. Sit!"

Angie's tone was so un-Angie-like, so stern, that Olivia was shocked. She sat.

"Now, for starters," Angie continued as Olivia perched uncomfortably on the edge of the bench, "Mrs. Engborg seems to feel you're extremely resistant to the new kids. And she can't figure it

145

out since just a few weeks ago you seemed okay. She seems to think you don't like the new kids, that you miss the old squad — maybe *too* much."

Olivia looked embarrassed and Angie felt so sorry she was putting her on the spot that she softened her voice and tried to show Olivia she understood.

"Look, I understand exactly how you must feel. After all, I was on Varsity for two years. I had to get used to new people each time. Last year I had to get used to *four* new people, *you* included. But I didn't look back at the previous year's squad. I worked to make the new squad the best ever because our school deserved it. You are still a terrific cheerleader, an outstanding gymnast — "

Olivia's chin came up at that and Angie knew she'd struck a nerve. Ardith had explained how Jessica now shared gymnastic stardom with Olivia and that she suspected Olivia's reaction to that was partly behind her lackluster performance.

"You know you can still be a star. You'll always be number one because you're the one with the most experience. If Ardith didn't consider experience to be so important she wouldn't have placed you in the position of captain, without a vote by the squad."

Olivia sat looking down at the floor, appearing to be unaffected by Angie's speech. Angie wanted to shake her.

"Olivia," she said, trying to infuse her voice with urgency. "You have to snap out of whatever it is that's got you locked up inside yourself. Stop

146

being so selfish. This new squad needs you. You have to set the pace. You've got to be their leader and stop thinking of any of them as being competition. Because *none* of them thinks of themselves as competition; they're just trying to be the best they can be."

Angie took Olivia's hand and squeezed it, willing Olivia to look at her.

Angie hadn't named Jessica, but Olivia knew she was thinking about her. How Angie realized that Olivia felt so clumsy and outclassed by Jessica, she wasn't sure. Perhaps she'd had a talk with Ardith about that. Ardith was such a good judge of character, such a great observer of people, perhaps she'd guessed. It was obvious everyone understood Olivia, and everyone expected her to "snap out of it." Why couldn't she seem to understand herself? And why did it seem so hard to snap out of it?

Olivia stirred, and mumbled, "Maybe you're right." She shrugged. "I don't know." She glanced at her watch. "But I do know that if I'm not home soon, my mother will call the police." She rose and picked up her gym bag. "It was great seeing you again," she told Angie, but the initial excitement she'd felt upon seeing her old squadmate for the first time had mellowed slightly.

Olivia felt as if a heavy weight were hampering her every move, and making her brain sluggish. "I really have to get home. You know how my mother is." She looked at Angie, her eyes blank and expressionless. She felt numb, as if she didn't know what to think or feel anymore.

Angie studied Olivia's face and sighed. In the past Olivia would never have used her mother as an excuse to do anything; she'd always ignored her. Angie reached out and hugged Olivia very tightly, wishing she could give Olivia some of her own life and enthusiasm. It pained and worried her to see Olivia like this! Hadn't anything she'd said to her sunk in? Wasn't there any way to reach her?

Ardith had said that depending on how Olivia performed her duties as captain at tomorrow's all-important game, she would either continue as captain, or Ardith would be forced to pick a new one. Ardith had made Angie promise not to reveal that to Olivia. Ardith wanted Olivia to perform naturally, without being forced to act simply to save her skin. After all, Ardith had had a talk with Olivia. Now it was up to Olivia.

Angie wanted so much to be able to motivate Olivia, to save her. If tomorrow Olivia failed to meet the coach's standards and she was removed as captain, Angie would feel like she'd been a failure, too.

"You want a lift home?" Angie asked.

Olivia hesitated. "No, thanks. I — I really feel the need to have some time to think. Alone." Her eyes begged for Angie's understanding.

"Yeah. Okay."

Angie watched Olivia turn and walk out of the locker room. She delayed her own departure a moment, gazing around at the room in which she, as a cheerleader for two years, had changed in and out of her red and white uniform. She reached

148

out and touched the cold metal of a nearby locker, and absentmindedly twirled the dial of the combination lock.

How many days and nights had she spent in this locker room, rejoicing over victories, and weeping over defeats? She missed the excitement, the almost painful anxiety before a game. Now life in college promised to be a new form of excitement along with hard work. But never again would she experience that unique emotional roller coaster that she'd known as a cheerleader. Those days were gone forever for her.

But Olivia still had time. She had a whole new year ahead of her. Maybe.

Don't blow it, Olivia, Angie thought and walked out of the locker room.

CHAPTER

 20

Olivia sat staring at the glass of orange juice sitting on the breakfast table in front of her as if it were a crystal ball. This afternoon would be the much-anticipated game against Garrison. Olivia wasn't sure she was up to it. She'd lain awake for a good portion of the night, thinking. One conclusion she'd drawn was that the only way she'd ever be able to feel good about herself again would be if she could prove she was as good as, if not better than, Jessica Bennett as a cheerleader and gymnast. In fact, she wanted to blow Jessica's performance away.

There were two ways she could prepare for the challenge. One was to practice fiendishly all this morning in her backyard. That wasn't a bad idea except for the fact that her mother would probably hover over her, yelling about not straining herself, not exerting herself. If Olivia didn't strain and exert, she wouldn't accomplish anything. Also, she needed Peter for a lot of the moves, since he was her gymnastics partner. Mrs. Engborg's choice of pairing up Peter and Olivia was based solely on size, not skill. Peter was smaller than Sean; Olivia was smaller than Jessica. When they performed identical maneuvers on the field, Jessica and Sean were at one end of the lineup, while Olivia and Peter were at the other, with Tara and Hope in between.

The only real objection to practicing all morning would be that Olivia could conceivably tire herself out so much she wouldn't have enough vitality left for a dazzling afternoon performance.

So that left the second plan as a superior alternative. It was for Olivia, as captain, to call for all the cheering routines that were the most strenuous, that would involve her and Jessica in the maximum amount of gymnastic moves. To pile one physically demanding routine on another would pit Olivia against Jessica, to see which of them had more stamina, more staying power. Olivia was pretty sure she'd come out on top. If there was one thing she had in her favor, it was a determination to stick to things, to last, to *endure*.

Also, she had an entire year of performing physically taxing cheerleading maneuvers behind her. Jessica didn't.

So Olivia opted for Plan B. She'd go to the game this afternoon and put the squad through its paces like never before. No one would object; they'd think she was pulling out all the stops for the benefit of the Wolves, to incite them to slaughter Garrison. And if that's what happened, then that would be icing on the cake.

Meanwhile she and Jessica would be locked in silent combat — even if only one of them was aware of it.

Olivia rose from the table, a determined lift to her chin. At the sound of the whistle, come out fighting. And may the best girl win!

The bleachers on either side of the football field were jam-packed. Wolves fans screamed lustily, though the game hadn't started. The teams hadn't even come out onto the field yet. The Garrison fans screamed right back. It looked to be an intense competition. Garrison had won its most recent game, while they were well aware of Tarenton's recent defeat at the hands of the Kensington Kings. They practically swaggered with the expectation of adding to Tarenton's list of losses.

The cheerleaders were loosely clustered in front of the stands. Olivia stood slightly apart, psyching herself up for the self-imposed ordeal ahead. She'd picked out the routines; she knew what to expect. That was to her advantage, since the others never knew what their captain might call. That was part of the privilege of being captain — assessing the situation at any point in the game and deciding which cheer to call.

Ardith studied Olivia. There was definitely a different aura about her today that had been missing lately. Even the way she paced a few steps back and forth seemed to signify unleashed energy. But her facial expression was unfamiliar to Ardith, and that worried her. She couldn't tell if it was an expression prompted by determination to give cheerleading all she had, to inspire the squad, or some other, darker, more disturbing emotion — an emotion that might even be destructive.

A movement at the edge of the field cut Ardith's musing short. The Tarenton players were beginning to stream out onto the field. Well whatever was going on beneath Olivia's surface, Ardith had the feeling she would soon find out what it was.

"Okay, squad," Olivia announced. "We're going to greet each player like he deserves! Jessica and I will stand on Sean's and Peter's shoulders, Tara and Hope do that pompon toss with us. Let's go!"

The squad looked momentarily surprised at this announcement for them to perform their most flamboyant team-greeting routine, then got into action.

The crowd got into the mood set by the cheerleaders and screamed themselves hoarse as each player was announced.

There was a temporary lull when all of the Wolves had been introduced, and it was Garrison's turn. The Garrison cheerleaders took over the cheering while Tarenton's squad rested temporarily on the lowest riser of the bleachers.

After the introductions were finished, the teams lined up for the first kickoff.

"All right, guys, let's do the 'Beat It' cheer," Olivia ordered, bounding to her feet.

The others lined up, but if any of them was wondering why she was calling that routine so early in the game, no one questioned it out loud.

Patrick and Pres showed up just seconds later. They'd been delayed by a moving job, but found that Angie and Christopher Page were sitting three rows behind the cheerleaders' spots and had saved them seats. Angie's eyes were riveted on Olivia, and she barely acknowledged the guys' arrival.

Was this the old Olivia, or some new, perhaps frightening one? Angie was asking herself as she watched Olivia cartwheel, flip, and catapult with an energy that seemed even more intense than last year.

Tara spotted Pres settling into his seat. She caught his eye and waved. He waved back, winked at her, and blew her a kiss. She raised one eyebrow and pursed her lips at him, returning the kiss. He'd dropped by last night and they'd ended up driving out along Fable Point where they'd parked and Pres had demonstrated his considerable expertise at kissing. Whereas Tara had been happy that it appeared Pres had forgotten the Pancake House episode from the previous Saturday, she'd returned home feeling a little unsettled. She hadn't been able to analyze it until Sean called, sounding irritated. He'd called while she'd been out and Marie had innocently told him Tara was with Pres. Sean had drawn his own, fairly

154

accurate conclusions, and hadn't been all that happy.

Tara decided that both guys were getting too possessive for her comfort, and along with that she was tiring of the war that was being waged between them. At first it had seemed like fun; now it was getting boring.

She glanced in Sean's direction and caught an envious look on his face.

Sean had seen Tara and Pres flirting — right in front of the whole school. He knew Pres was recognized, and that kiss he'd blown Tara stamped her as his, at least in the minds of the observers.

Sean was fed up. How was he ever going to get Pres off the scene and have Tara to himself?

Olivia called for their combination cheer, the one Ardith had devised from elements of each cheerleader's contribution.

"Come on, Wolves — show 'em your bite!"

Perfect, Sean thought. I'll just add a little pizzazz to my part of the routine. That ought to impress Tara.

The cheerleaders yelled out the chant, and right after placing his megaphone down, Sean turned his *back* to Jessica, cupping his hands behind him. She stared at the stirrup he was forming behind his back and knew that it was all wrong. But obviously this was a deliberate action on his part. She was too professional to cop out of the routine, so she placed her foot in the stirrup, and hoped Sean had the strength in this position to send her vaulting up and over into a back flip.

Thankfully he did, and the maneuver worked.

When it was all over, Tara looked at him with discomfort, as they took a short break and headed for their bench.

"What was that for, Dubrow?" Peter asked. "Why did you do it backward?"

Sean shrugged and said, "Just adding a little class. That's all."

"What if you hadn't had the lift to get Jessica up and over? She'd have fallen in a heap!" Peter continued, irritated at Sean's lack of respect for doing things by the rules.

"Hey, no sweat." Sean made a muscle close to Tara's face.

Peter rolled his eyes. "Hey, Sean, quit playing macho man and do the cheers right. You can pursue your love life later — when no one can get hurt."

"Buzz off, Rayman. I'm in control," Sean told him arrogantly.

Tara frowned. It was one thing to have a guy showing off for you. But it was another if his showing off could really hurt someone else. Tara studied Sean covertly, debating with herself. She suddenly felt ashamed . . . and frightened.

Meanwhile, out on the field, the energy level was at an all-time high. Both teams seemed to regard this as mortal combat rather than sport. Throughout the first quarter of the game, neither team scored, and then at the start of the second quarter, Garrison got a touchdown.

Olivia sprang into action. "Come on, squad. Time for the new 'Victory or Bust' cheer!"

Peter took his spot next to Olivia, finding himself actually out of breath from the last cheer, which they'd only completed a few minutes before this call.

"What's with you, Olivia?" he wondered out loud. "Are we cheering or trying to kill ourselves?"

"What's the matter? Is cheerleading too strenuous for you?" Olivia retorted, and then found herself feeling contrite for snapping at Peter. She had no quarrel with him; he didn't deserve her ire. "Sorry," she apologized quickly, as the squad lined up. "Guess I'm just out to win." Peter didn't have to know she was talking about her own private contest.

Sean took his position at the opposite end of the squad lineup from Peter. His thoughts were also the opposite from Peter's. He was impressed with Olivia's spunk today. She was being more like the kind of captain he felt the squad deserved. It was obvious to him that she wanted to get the fans up to an incredibly high energy level and then keep them there. And he was all for it. In fact, it just occurred to him that *this* routine she'd called was the perfect one for showcasing that fancy key-catching maneuver he'd invented. His megaphone stood two feet away from him and he knew the exact spot in the routine where he'd be free to step over, grab it, and toss it in the air. He'd dazzle everyone — and prove to Tara beyond the shadow of a doubt that he was a better cheerleader than Preston Tilford III had ever even dreamed of being.

"Get set!" Olivia called the first two words of the cheer and the squad moved into action.

> "Get set to win!
> To pound them thin. . . ."

The squad chanted and performed the energetic footwork. It was fashioned after rock 'n' roll dancing, with Peter and Olivia at one end, Jessica and Sean at the other. The two couples performed in synchronization while Tara and Hope called the chant out to the crowd. First the guys swung the girls out under their arms, and the girls pirouetted and were flung back to their original starting positions. At this point the guys were to do spread-eagle jumps, touching their toes with their fingertips, while the girls stepped out to do two back flips. Then Peter and Sean were supposed to catch Olivia and Jessica as they ended their second flips against the guys' arms, which were to wrap around the girls to steady them at their waists.

But Sean didn't do his leap. Jessica, concentrating on her flips, and facing away from him, didn't notice. Instead, he stepped forward, grabbbed his megaphone, and tossed it into the air behind him. He tried to use just the right force and angle to make it come down right behind his back as he stepped backward and caught it.

Unfortunately he hadn't practiced this maneuver, and he overthrew the megaphone. It forced him to take two steps back, where he did manage to catch it before setting it down. But now he was one pace away from the spot where Jessica was landing, expecting to find Sean's supporting arm to steady her.

He leaped forward but his arm slipped down around her hips, and Jessica fell backward, now doing an unrehearsed back flip right over his arm.

She saw the ground coming ʼup to meet her and thought: I'm going to fall and break my neck!

Years of gymnastic practice came to her rescue. Instinctively her arms shot out and her hands hit the ground to break her fall. Then to cover up the blunder, instantly, miraculously, she did a handspring up and back onto her feet again. She stood there, dazed, her brain muddled as it tried to sort out what had happened during the last thirty seconds.

The crowd, unaware that Jessica and Sean were supposed to have been perfroming the exact same moves as Olivia and Peter, cheered.

Olivia, who hadn't witnessed the action from her position at the other end of the lineup, glanced down at Sean and Jessica and saw that Jessica was standing in the wrong place. Instead of Sean being on the end, Jessica was. And she and Sean were fully two paces off their spots. The rest of the routine dictated that the entire squad do walkovers followed by forward cartwheels. But if Jessica were to do that, she'd smash right into the Wolves' players' bench.

In lightning speed Olivia's mind registered two facts. Number one, Jessica was looking pale and stunned. Obviously she was beginning to feel the hard workout Olivia had devised. Olivia should have felt exonerated, triumphant. But the second fact percolating through her mind eclipsed that: Because Jessica was in such a state, she didn't appear to notice that when they went into the next segment of the routine, she would crash into the hard wooden bench. She'd never do that without being hurt — maybe seriously. And all because of this ridiculous vendetta of mine! Olivia realized with self-loathing.

What a terrible person I am! she thought. This was all *my* fault. Captains were not supposed to cause the squad members to be hurt.

The five other cheerleaders were, at that moment, waiting uneasily for her signal for them to begin the walkovers. Before anyone could react, Olivia stepped forward, clapped, and jumped in place so she was facing down the lineup. She threw her body into a series of cartwheels, wheeling past the startled faces of Hope, Tara, and Sean. She landed directly in front of Jessica, clapped, and jumped in place so she was facing Jessica, with her back to the crowd.

"Jessica," she whispered. "Get over on the other side of Sean. You'll hit the players' bench."

Without waiting to see if Jessica did as she was told, Olivia clapped and jump-turned again, performing two more cartwheels back down to her end of the lineup and hopping into her place.

By now the other four members realized just what she'd done. She'd saved Jessica from certain injury and had done it in an inspired series of moves that had made it look like the whole thing had been part of the original routine.

"And go!" Olivia said, breathing heavily.

The six did walkovers, followed by the cartwheels. And no one was hurt. Sean missed the end of the players' bench by inches, but still he missed it.

The crowd went crazy with foot stomping and cheering. The cheerleaders stood before them, smiling in relief. Disaster had been averted, and no one in the stands even knew.

Then the halftime whistle blew and the squad collapsed onto the risers.

People flowed around them like lava, heading for the refreshment stands. With Garrison ahead, the teams retreated to their locker rooms to prepare for the second half of the game.

Olivia started as she felt someone place a hand on her shoulder. She was even more surprised when she looked up and saw it was Jessica.

CHAPTER

21

Jessica sank down on the bench beside Olivia and said in an earnest voice, "Thanks a lot, Olivia. You saved me out there."

"It's okay," Olivia answered, feeling embarrassed. If Jessica even guessed what a turmoil Olivia had been in over her!

As if Jessica had the ability to read minds, she went on, though sounding hesitant and unsure of Olivia's reaction to her next words. "You know, I guess it kind of surprised me. The way you've been for the past few weeks, I almost would have expected you to just let me crash into that bench." She lightened her words with a wide smile. "But in retrospect I guess your saving me is exactly what I *should* have expected. You're a real pro, and the squad always comes first." She fixed her green gaze on Olivia.

"You know," Jessica continued, "that's what I

162

always admired about you last year. I could tell that for you, the squad's performance was the most important activity whenever you guys were out there cheering." She gave Olivia a brief, spontaneous hug and said simply, "So thanks again for saving me from breaking every bone in my body." She laughed nervously and waited for Olivia's reaction.

Olivia returned the laugh a little stiffly, and looked down at the pompon she was absent-mindedly twirling in her hands. "You're welcome, Jessica. And thanks for being open and honest with me. You know, I realize you've just hit the nail on the head. In the end, the squad *did* come first with me. And that's the way it's going to be now."

She glanced in Jessica's direction, feeling too uptight to look directly into her clear, green eyes. "I hate to admit it, but I was having a rough time adjusting to the new squad. It was stupid, but that's what it was." This time she did have the courage to look at Jessica. "But that's *over*. From now on I'm concentrating on shaping up our *new* squad and making it the best ever!"

Jessica smiled widely at her and gave her another fierce hug. "Oh, Olivia, I'm so glad to hear that! I'll be right there behind you all the way."

"Great," Olivia said with relief, glad she could put to rest the ridiculous and unjust antagonism she'd felt toward Jessica.

Her glance strayed to just over Jessica's shoulder, and she saw Hope sitting alone temporarily. "And while I'm setting things right, there's another item of unfinished business I have to take care of. Excuse me." She rose and headed straight for Hope.

Peter was nowhere in sight. Olivia guessed he might have gone off for refreshments.

Hope was staring around her, looking a bit lonesome.

"Hi," Olivia said, walking over to sit next to Hope.

Hope's dark eyes widened as she looked at Olivia in surprise and said, "Hi."

"Listen," Olivia began, again experiencing a knot in her stomach like she'd had when talking to Jessica. How come righting wrongs caused so much pain? She cleared her throat and tried again. "Look, I want to apologize if I've been remote or preoccupied in the past few weeks. A couple of things happened to me personally, but I've got a handle on them now. And I just wanted you to know I remember how it feels to be the only junior on a senior-dominated Varsity Squad. But you blend in beautifully. You'll do fine. And if there's anything I can do to make it easier for you, please tell me." She looked at Hope and saw pleasure transform Hope's face almost magically.

"Oh, thanks, Olivia. Maybe I will." Her glance shifted and Olivia turned to see Peter approaching with two cups of cold soda. She smiled back at Hope.

"But I don't think you'll need my help," she teased. "Looks like someone else has already volunteered for the job."

Hope blushed and covered her mouth with her hands.

Olivia rose, still smiling, and turned toward the stands. The smile faded as she saw Patrick gazing down at Jessica. Jessica was, at the moment, talking to some guys who were grouped around her — admirers. Now, while there was still some halftime remaining, Olivia decided she was going to take care of one more thing that was bothering her.

Quickly she made her way to Patrick's side and put a hand on his wide, strong shoulder.

"Hey, Patrick. How's it going?"

He looked up at her, and smiled. "Just great. You guys were spectacular. You sure put on one heck of a display."

"Yeah, I guess we did." Olivia sat down on the spot vacated by Pres, who'd gone off to the refreshment stand. "Patrick," she began seriously, "I have to talk to you about something."

Patrick frowned slightly at the somber tone in her voice. "Yeah? About what?"

"Jessica."

Patrick's frown deepened and he seemed to withdraw mentally from Olivia. "Oh, yeah? What about her?"

"Jessica's a nice girl; don't get me wrong. But I'm worried about you and — and her. Patrick, she's not interested in a permanent relationship with any guy. She told Tara that in the locker room. Please be careful. I'd hate for you to end up in another dead-end relationship."

She hadn't said Mary Ellen's name, but Patrick was perfectly aware that she was implying that that was exactly what he'd had with her.

"Well, thanks, small stuff, for caring." Patrick pretended to box Olivia's chin. "But I can take care of myself." He sent her one of his lopsided grins. "Besides, I'm beginning to think I just go for the wrong girls. Some guys do." He leaned back, resting casually against the riser behind him.

Olivia stared at him, not sure if he was putting on an act. Then she decided he was telling the truth.

"You're sincere," she finally said, jumping up to give him a kiss on the cheek. "That's why I like you so much." She turned her head and saw the halftime clock. "Oops! Gotta go if I want a drink before we have to start cheering again."

Down at the bottom of the stands Tara was talking to Sean.

"Look, try to contain all that machismo during the second half, will you? If you kill Jessica we'll have to find a replacement."

"Hey, I was just proving who was the better cheerleader," Sean defended.

"Of whom? You or Peter? Or you and Pres?" She didn't let Sean answer. She was tired of a game that had gotten out of hand and endangered a fellow cheerleader. "I realize what you're trying to do, but you're trying too hard. You should be directing all that energy and effort toward winning a girl who'll be crazy about you. I'm sorry, but I'm not that girl. In fact, I'm not about to get serious about any guy. Hey, I'm just out to have fun. I can see you need a girl who'll be yours exclusively. You and Pres are making me feel tied down, walled in. It's time for me to move on."

She glanced at the players who were trotting back out onto the field from beside the bleachers. "In fact, I've got a date after the game with Rex Granger. So you're both free as little birds to find someone else."

With that Tara patted Sean on the shoulder and walked over to where the other cheerleaders were beginning to cluster, gearing up for the second half.

Tara decided she'd gotten out of that okay. Both guys were just getting too close. And Tara didn't want any guy to get close enough to see through her veneer, to see that down deep inside she was a great big zero. As long as they saw the glittery surface, she was happy. No one would ever like her if they saw beneath it. And by telling Sean he and Pres were a part of her past, she probably had managed to save Jessica from further misfortune during the second half. I'm not half bad, Tara thought, smiling.

Sean closed his mouth when he realized he'd been staring after Tara with it open. He'd been dumped! In fact, both he *and* Pres had been dumped. It was beyond belief. Tara was perfectly serious about it, too. He could tell she hadn't been putting him on. He stuffed his hands in his pants pockets and realized that Tara had even moved on to another guy already.

But strangely, Sean realized he wasn't exactly broken up about it. Maybe that was because he knew Pres wasn't going to get Tara, either. The two of them would just have to look for someone else.

Sean sauntered forward, heading for the cheerleaders.

So, okay, Tara was old news. There were plenty of girls dying to take her place. In fact, during the second half of the game he'd just scan the crowd and pick out the very one he'd move in on right after the game. No point in wasting time.

The sweep of his gaze took in Pres, who was standing at the bottom of the stands, waiting for a break in the flow of people so he could mount the steps back to his seat.

Now comes the fun part, Sean thought gleefully. Before Pres could get away Sean collared him.

"Hey, Pres, old man. Guess what? We've just been dumped by a luscious redhead."

Pres looked at him in confusion. "What?"

"Tara, man, She just told *both* of us to take a hike. Seems she and Rex Granger will be the next hot item."

Right then, as if to illustrate this, Rex came over to Tara and picked her up, twirling her around. He set her down and she laughed up at him.

"So, fella, guess she's dumped us both," Sean said, laughing. "I for one will have no problem filling her spot." He glanced around, winked at the first girl to catch his eye, and then sighed deeply. "Nope. No problem at all. Let me know if you need any help. I've got an awesome little black book." With that he sauntered over to re-join the squad.

Pres dropped into his seat next to Patrick. What a set-up! He'd been played by a master of the game. He'd been so sure of Tara, and had she ever taken the wind out of his sails! He shook his head and watched the rest of the game in a daze.

The second half of the game was sensational. Not only did the squad put on a brilliant show under Olivia's leadership, but the Wolves performed like never before, wiping out Garrison with a victory of twenty-one to six. When the final whistle blew, people raced out onto the field to hoist the Wolves up on their shoulders.

Tara ran out to Rex Granger, who picked her up and carried her on his lap as he was borne off the field by six excited fans. She'd made a play for Rex right after halftime had begun, and had wrangled a date out of him before she'd had the showdown with Sean. Tara had no idea if she intended to start up with Rex, who'd been an obvious admirer of hers for some time. But she was just sure she wasn't going to play Sean off against Pres, or anyone, ever again. It was too dangerous.

Peter picked up Hope and squeezed her. "We did it! Now we can celebrate!" He grabbed her hand as he set her down and the two of them ran, laughing together in pure joy, off to change in the locker rooms.

Patrick approached Jessica hesitantly. She looked up at him and smiled. He took that as a positive sign and said in a voice full of confidence he wasn't sure he was feeling, "So where to after you change?"

"The Pizza Palace, of course," Jessica said without hesitation. She smiled up at Patrick, threaded her arm through his, and the two of them followed the crowd flowing away from the field.

Just like Mary Ellen, Patrick thought, smiling to himself. One minute aloof, one minute friendly.

He's really so nice, Jessica thought. There's no harm in seeing him. I won't get too involved.

Sean was descended upon by about six girls, and found a likely candidate for his attentions, he decided, as he spied a pretty blonde girl with deep blue eyes and a shy smile. "What's your name, beautiful?"

She laughed and the group moved as one, escorting Sean off the field.

Olivia picked up her pompons and spied Angie and Christopher standing at the base of the bleachers. Angie's beautiful smile was aimed straight at Olivia.

Olivia trotted over to her, greeting her with a bear hug.

"You were wonderful, Olivia. You are *really* the captain now," Angie said. Her eyes were suspiciously moist.

"Thanks." Olivia felt extremely humbled by

what she'd experienced today. "You were right, you know. And so was Mrs. Engborg. From now on I'm really going to work on making the new squad a cohesive group — maybe even friends — no matter what happens in the months ahead. I'm going to try to be the very best captain Varsity could have this year."

"Oh, Livvy! I'm so happy to hear that," Angie said. "And I'm so excited about the year ahead for you. So many things can happen. This is your last year on Varsity, so make the most of it."

"I intend to," Olivia assured her, linking arms with Angie. They began walking off the field.

What kind of things could happen this year? Olivia wondered. Would they be good, or bad, or a little of both? Well, it didn't do any good to speculate about it. She'd just have to wait and see.

What have the cheerleaders got against Olivia's new boyfriend? Read Cheerleaders #23, PROVING IT.

If you have enjoyed reading this book in the exciting CHEERLEADERS series look out for the other titles also available now:

COMING SOON